Also by John Boyne

NOVELS

The Thief of Time

The Congress of Rough Riders

Crippen

Next of Kin

Mutiny on the Bounty

The House of Special Purpose

The Absolutist

This House is Haunted

A History of Loneliness

The Heart's Invisible Furies

A Ladder to the Sky

A Traveller at the Gates of Wisdom

The Echo Chamber

All the Broken Places

NOVELS FOR YOUNGER READERS

The Boy in the Striped Pyjamas

Noah Barleywater Runs Away

The Terrible Thing That Happened to Barnaby Brocket

Stay Where You Are and Then Leave

The Boy at the Top of the Mountain

My Brother's Name is Jessica

NOVELLAS

The Second Child

The Dare

SHORT STORIES

Beneath the Earth

Water

www.penguin.co.uk

Water

JOHN BOYNE

doubleday

TRANSWORLD PUBLISHERS
Penguin Random House, One Embassy Gardens,
8 Viaduct Gardens, London SW11 7BW
www.penguin.co.uk

Transworld is part of the Penguin Random House group of companies
whose addresses can be found at global.penguinrandomhouse.com

First published in Great Britain in 2023 by Doubleday
an imprint of Transworld Publishers

A CIP catalogue record for this book
is available from the British Library.

ISBNs
9780857529817 (hb)
9780857529800 (tpb)

Typeset in 11/14.5pt Dante MT Std by Jouve (UK), Milton Keynes
Printed and bound in India by Replika Press Pvt. Ltd.

The authorized representative in the EEA is Penguin Random House Ireland,
Morrison Chambers, 32 Nassau Street, Dublin D02 YH68.

Penguin Random House is committed to a sustainable future
for our business, our readers and our planet. This book is made
from Forest Stewardship Council® certified paper.

In memory of Michael Grimley,
and for Carmel

I

THE FIRST THING I do when I arrive on the island is change my name.

I've been Vanessa Carvin for a long time, twenty-eight years, but I was Vanessa Hale for twenty-four years before that and there's an unexpected comfort in reclaiming my birthright, which sometimes feels as if it was stolen from me, even though I was complicit in the crime.

A few minutes later, I change it again, this time to Willow Hale. Willow is my middle name, and it seems prudent to take a further step in separating the woman I am now from the woman I once was, lest anyone here makes the connection. My parents were unremarkable, middle-class people – a teacher and a shop assistant – and there were some who thought them presumptuous in calling their daughter Vanessa Willow, which summons images of a Bloomsbury writer or a painter's wan muse, but I was always rather pleased with it. I had notions about myself back then, I suppose. I don't have them any longer.

My next task is to shave my head. I've kept my hair shoulder length and blonde for as long as I can remember but I purchased an electric razor before leaving Dublin and plug the device in to charge for half an hour before easing it around my skull, experiencing a feverish delight in watching the clumps tumble into the sink or fall on the floor around my feet. Standing in the cascading tendrils of my femininity, I decide not to make myself entirely bald for that would draw too much attention, and I don't have the head for it anyway, unlike the famous singer who looked like one of God's angels when she first appeared on our television screens. Instead, I shear myself down to the uncomplicated blunt crop of a hard-working country woman, someone far too busy to concern herself with indulging the physical. The blonde is gone now, replaced by a darkish grey that must have been lurking inside me all the time, like a benign cancer. I wonder how I will look when it starts to grow out again and rather hope that it won't. The truth is, it would be more convenient if it just gave up the ghost with the cruel efficiency it inflicts on men.

I explore the cottage and find it suitable to my needs. The photographs I saw online did not lie about its austerity. The front door opens on to a living room that houses a kitchen. Or, perhaps, a kitchen that houses a living room. There's a single bedroom with a single bed – how strange it will feel to sleep like a child again – and a small bathroom with no shower. An unappealing rubber attachment is squeezed plumply around the tap spouts, and I pull it away, relocating it to a cupboard beneath the sink. The roof must be sound for there are no damp spots on the stone floor that have fallen from above. The simplicity, the monastic nature of all of this, pleases me. It is so far from what I am accustomed to.

When I first made enquiries of the owner, a man named Peadar Dooley, I asked about the Wi-Fi, and he told me a pub on the island offered it but that very few of the houses had access yet and his was not one of them.

'I suppose that'll rule the place out for you?' he asked, disappointment in his tone, for this was not the type of cottage to draw many offers, and certainly not for an open-ended lease.

'On the contrary,' I told him. 'If anything, it makes it more appealing.'

When I turn on the taps, the water emerges brown at first before clearing its throat in the pipes and running clear. I place my hand beneath it, and it is shockingly cold. Taking a glass from the shelf, I fill it and drink. I cannot remember when I last experienced such purity. I drink more and feel something inside me spring to life. I wonder, could a person get drunk on this water?

Moving from room to room, I check the light switches and am relieved that they're all in working order since the island at night is sure to be darker than any place I've ever known. The wallpaper is bleached of its colour and looks as if it remains on the wall out of habit more than anything else; one good tug, however, and I imagine the sheets would fall away without complaint. Something is missing and it takes me a few moments to realize what it is: there is no television set. I'm not disappointed. If I am to live this hermetic existence, then it is best that nothing intrudes upon it. It will be a rare privilege to be so wilfully ignorant of the outside world and all its nonsense.

There is, however, a radio, an old-fashioned one with

an aerial folded down. I turn it on but receive only static. Pulling up the copper spike, I rotate the dial and soon find myself tuned in to RTÉ Radio 1, where Joe Duffy is displaying admirable patience while interrogating one of his listeners about the latest indignity that has befallen her. For years, I listened to Joe's show every day, but I turn it off now. Over the last twelve months, Brendan and I were the subject of debate on many occasions and, masochist that I am, I couldn't stop myself from obsessively listening as strangers called in to denounce us both.

'And as for her,' they would say, vicious in their moral superiority. 'Sure, you only have to look at that creature to see that she was in on it all along. Like attracts like.'

I've sworn that I won't pay attention to these merciless commentators any more and so I remove the batteries from the device and bury them in different parts of the back garden, smoothing over their graves so I won't be able to find them again.

Food. That will be an issue. The taxi driver, the only one on the island, a man named Mícheál Óg Ó'Ceallaigh, brought me and my suitcase from the dock to the cottage and told me there was a 'grand little shop' only twenty minutes' walk from where I would be staying, between the pub and the church. The old pub, he added, not the new pub. I shall enjoy walking. They say that exercise is good for one's mental health, and mine is in a low place. Right now, however, I'm not hungry, and, even if I was, Mr Dooley must have an agent somewhere nearby, for a fresh loaf of bread has been left on the table and there's butter, ham, eggs and cheese in the fridge, as well as a small sack of potatoes slumped like a weary traveller by the front door.

When I unpack my suitcase, I'm surprised to find that I included a toiletries bag bursting with make-up, the zip straining against the pressure of a lifetime's commitment to hiding the truth. I don't remember including it. Perhaps it was simply an unconscious gesture after years of packing for holidays and Brendan's work trips. I spill its contents on to the bed now and look them over. There must be a thousand euros' worth of deception here, promises of youth decanted into white tubes, glass bottles and plastic containers. I sweep the lot back into the bag and throw it all in the bin. Rebecca, my younger daughter, would have a fit if she witnessed such waste. Some years ago, when she was fourteen, she turned into something of an eco-warrior and was forever scolding me for throwing things away when there was still life in them, just as men do with their first wives. Anyway, it's no longer an issue for I intend to embrace a plain complexion here. I'll wash my face with soap, dry it with a rough towel, and let the elements do their worst.

I didn't bring many clothes, so it doesn't take long for me to hang them up in the wardrobe. A few pairs of jeans. Some T-shirts. Underwear. A couple of heavy woollen jumpers. I anticipated the Atlantic cold and rather liked the idea of walking along the cliffs like an actress in a television advertisement, staring out to sea and contemplating the ruins of my existence. Only two pairs of shoes. The ones I'm wearing, which are really just a comfortable pair of trainers, and a second pair that aren't much better. I should have brought some hiking boots, I suppose. I wonder if there might be a place to purchase some here as I have no intention of returning to the mainland during my self-imposed exile. If not, I will simply have to survive with what I have. People always used to. Plenty still have no choice.

The front door is ajar, and a cat marches in, pausing for a moment in surprise, her front right paw held in mid-air. She stares at me in outrage as if I, and not she, is the intruder.

'I have a rental agreement,' I tell her, and her eyes narrow at my insolence. 'Do you want to see it?'

I'm not much of an animal person and hope that she'll take umbrage at this infringement of her rights and leave, but no, she simply emits a resigned miaow before making her way to the armchair and springing on to it before promptly falling asleep. Emma, my elder daughter, wanted a dog when she was a child, but Brendan claimed to be allergic, another assertion I never really believed. The truth was that he valued order and felt that having any sort of pet around the place would lead to chaos. Toys everywhere. Baskets. Water bowls. Urine on the floor tiles. I regret that now. We only have our children with us for a short time. It seems churlish not to give them the things they ask for, particularly when they're asking for something that might love them unconditionally.

I allow my mind to drift to my ex-husband for a moment. Well, he's surrounded by chaos now, I tell myself, wondering whether I should smile at the irony but being unable to. Although he's technically not my ex-husband at all yet. I just think of him that way. One day, I will summon the energy to speak to a solicitor but, right now, I have had enough of the legal system to last me a lifetime, and who knows, maybe he'll die, or be killed, which would save me both the bother and the expense.

With nothing left to do in the cottage, I step back outside and look around. It is a fine day, neither cold nor warm, without even the whisper of a breeze in the air. There are a few other houses in sight, each one located at some distance from mine. A dozen or more cattle and sheep dot the fields of my closest neighbour, whose farmhouse stands atop a hill, perhaps ten minutes' walk from my door. 'This is where I live now,' I say aloud, and my voice doesn't sound like my own. Perhaps it's something in the island acoustics, an inharmonious meeting point between water, earth, fire and air. It's hard to believe that I've landed in such a place.

Earlier, on a whim, I checked the calendar on my phone to see where I'd been on this day last year and it turned out to have been the morning that Brendan and I had an audience with Pope Francis in Rome. The Irish Ambassador to the Holy See had introduced us, telling His Holiness that this was the great Brendan Carvin, who was known and admired the length and breadth of the country, and if Brendan had been blessed with feathers, he would have spread them wide and enclosed us all within his colourful train. And this is his wife, the ambassador added a moment later, not deeming me worthy of a name, and I performed a sort of curtsey in the black dress I'd bought for the occasion in Brown Thomas, which hung between my knees and ankles, my face hidden behind a veil, presumably to protect the Pope from any temptation.

Francis's was not the first papal hand that either Brendan or I had shaken – there were two others – but it will certainly be the last.

I look at my watch. Three o'clock now and already I'm not sure how I'll fill the rest of the day. I've brought a few books with me – classics, mostly – but amn't in the mood for reading. I'll go to the shop, I suppose. Explore. Build up an appetite and see what they serve in the pub, assuming they have a menu at all. Maybe I'll get drunk and dance on a table. It would be quite something to be barred from one of the island's two pubs on my first night here.

I remember my phone now and go back inside to retrieve it from my handbag, touching the screen to bring it to life and, to my surprise, I have five full bars. So, no Wi-Fi, but plenty of coverage. Opening my messaging service, I scroll to Rebecca's name, rereading our last conversation, which took place more than a week ago, and glance towards the top of the screen. With no regard for her privacy, it tells me that she is online.

I've arrived, I tell her. *I'm on the island.* And then, despite having no reason to believe this, I add: *I think you'd like it here.*

I send the message and watch as a grey tick appears next to it, then another. A moment later, they turn blue. She's reading it. A rare moment when I know exactly what my daughter is doing.

The word *typing* . . . appears below.

She's replying.

But then it disappears.

She's changed her mind.

The picture on her profile vanishes too. I know what this means. That she has blocked me. Temporarily, at least. She does this quite regularly, usually in the immediate aftermath of my contacting her, but I always wake the next day to find her picture restored.

I set the phone down on the table. There is only one more thing I need to do before I head to the village and that is to take the small, framed photograph of Emma, Rebecca and me from my suitcase and place it on the table, in full view of the sofa. It was taken years ago when the girls were ten and eight respectively. Brendan isn't in it, of course. If he had been, I'd have burned it. But he remains a presence, after a fashion, for he must have been the person behind the camera. I consider smashing the frame on the floor and tearing the photograph to shreds, because of his ghostly presence, but if I do this, then I will have no pictures of my daughters at all. True, Rebecca will have restored hers by tomorrow morning but there'll be no more of Emma in this lifetime. My failures as a mother have ensured that.

'What do you think?' I ask the cat, who opens a lazy eye and, as if rethinking her earlier fearlessness, leaps from the armchair and marches out the door. I'm not far behind her.

2

It doesn't take long for the people of the island to become intrigued by the stranger who has appeared in their midst. I suppose they rarely encounter outsiders, except during the summer months when the tourists arrive, a prospect I'm already dreading. Holidaymakers from Dublin, after all, might recognize me, so I will need to keep my wits about me then. I'm conscious of my arrogance in assuming that no one on this small atoll could possibly identify me, but I feel reasonably confident that they won't.

A rumour spreads that a woman from the mainland, which usually means Galway, Mayo, or Clare, has rented Peadar Dooley's cottage and, in each shop I enter, I am asked to confirm that I am the refugee in question. When I do, I'm greeted with a mixture of excitement, alarm, and, above all, concern for my safety. The general feeling is that my new home is not sufficiently insulated and that, if I remain there, I will surely die from hypothermia.

'It's actually quite warm,' I tell the fifth or sixth islander to prophesy my demise and my Cassandra is preparing to contradict me, to assure me that I'll be dead within the month, when her husband interrupts to say that no, the Dooley cottage was constructed with good bricks.

'Most aren't,' he observes, scratching his stubbly chin. There is more hair growing from his ears, nose and eyebrows than from his head, and it's a disconcerting sight. 'Not any more. And cheap blocks will let the cold in every time. But a cottage with good bricks? They'll protect you. Do you know himself at all?'

'Who?' I ask.

'Your man Dooley.'

'No,' I tell him, shaking my head. 'We conducted our business over email. He doesn't live here, I believe.'

'Away across,' he replies, nodding in the general direction of Ireland. ''Twas his father, Shay Dooley, built that cottage. Put it together with his own hands. People did, back then. Now, they wouldn't know how. Sure, the old skills are long gone.'

I'm trying to imagine the work that must have gone into the construction. Where did the bricks even come from? Or the mortar? How deep are the foundations? And, while he was about it, would it have killed him to have installed a shower?

'You're a writer, I bet,' says the woman, with a confident smile on her face. 'I'd put a pound to a penny that you are.'

'Why do you say that?' I ask.

'It's the sort of thing writers do, isn't it?' she says. 'They rent some oul' cottage in the middle of nowhere when they're working on a book and then off they feck when the thing is finished and go on Pat Kenny or Ryan

Tubridy to tell everyone listening how the place changed them. I'm right, amn't I?'

'I'm afraid not,' I say, amused by the idea. I have a story to tell, it's true, but I lack the inclination to tell it.

She seems disappointed, as if she had hoped that I was importing a little celebrity to island life and I have thwarted her. Perhaps she envisioned lectures or workshops. A reading in the church. A book group. Anything that would alter the monotony of her daily existence.

'Then what is it you do?' she asks, irritated now, as if I'm being deliberately obtuse by not being a writer.

'I don't do anything,' I tell her.

'But before you came here? You must have done something.'

'No, nothing at all,' I reply, and I hear how ridiculous this sounds, but, after all, it's the truth. I did nothing. I'm an able-bodied, intellectually curious woman of fifty-two years who hasn't drawn a pay cheque in almost three decades. What a thing to admit.

Still, for all their prying, I enjoy talking to the islanders. They are, for the most part, a friendly group. And, whatever curiosity they feel, they have the decency not to ask too many questions about why I have exchanged a city of around one and a half million people for an island of four hundred. I had expected more of an inquisition. One or two extract the information that I am from Dublin, and they wrap their arms around themselves then, shaking their heads in wariness, as if they've heard nothing but bad about that place and would no more visit it than journey to the moon.

I develop a routine to my days. I wake at seven and take a long walk along the cliffs, enjoying the feeling of the early-morning wind in my face, before returning to the cottage, where I eat a light breakfast and check when Rebecca was last online. I feel a sense of relief when I see that it was relatively early – say around eleven p.m. – but much later than that and I start to worry. On the rare occasions when I see that she was still using her phone at three or four o'clock in the morning, I grow concerned and wonder what she might be doing. Is there a boy, perhaps, keeping her awake? She's never liked to confide in me about her romantic life but, aged twenty-four, it would be perverse if she hadn't had some experiences in that area. I've only met one who might have been considered a suitor, and that was the young man who took her to her Debs six years ago. Colm, or Colin, or Colum. Something like that. A face still troubled by acne, with a mop of shiny red hair and an air of uncertainty about him. Thin, bony fingers. Brendan behaved as if he was Spencer Tracy in *Father of the Bride*, all gruff and authoritative, but the part didn't suit him. Colm, or Colin, or Colum told me that he wanted to be an entomologist and I think I surprised him, disappointed him even, when I knew what that word meant and he didn't have the pleasure of explaining it to me. It was a job, I thought, that would suit him. Anyway, I never saw him again after the Debs and, if I raised his name, Rebecca would pretend she didn't know who I was talking about.

I have occasionally wondered whether she might be more interested in girls than boys, but no, on reflection, I don't think that's the case. I've noticed her, in unguarded moments, casting glances towards handsome men in shops or restaurants and, anyway, she's not the type to hide a marginal sexuality, as if it was something shameful. If anything, she would revel in it. And she knows it wouldn't matter to me in the slightest who she brought home, although, if I'm honest, I'd prefer it was a boy, just to keep things simple. I'm aware that expressing a sentiment like that can get a person in trouble these days, but life, I feel, is hard enough without adding another layer of difficulty. And to be fair to Brendan, I think he would have felt the same way. Although, whatever she is, he won't be the one walking her up the aisle, should such a day ever come.

And Emma, of course, died before she could fall in love with anyone, so there are no stories there.

The mornings pass quickly. I take a bath, washing my head by submerging myself in the water and blocking out the silence. I clean things that I cleaned the day before. I talk to the cat, who has grudgingly accepted my presence but will not be denied her armchair. I read. I look out the window. I think about the morning when the Gardaí arrived at our front door in Terenure. I tell myself not to think about the morning when the Gardaí arrived at our front door in Terenure. And, in this way, the hours pass and, before I know it, it's almost lunchtime and I can walk down to the village.

There's not much to do there but it's important to get out and speak to people, not to be seen as the mad Dublin woman hiding out in the cottage above. Also, I have a fear that if I am seen as a recluse, some well-meaning but pushy neighbour will invite me for dinner and then I'll be passed from house to house till they strip the past out of me and I'll have no choice but to up sticks and move again. No, better to be seen as available but stand-offish. Whenever I notice one of the islanders looking in my direction, I smile and engage them in conversation. The weather, of course, for where would we all be without conversations about it? The longer stretch in the evenings. The possibility of a storm. They talk of the tides, of their unpredictable ways, but I know little of this subject, even if it does fascinate me.

I go to the new pub for lunch – a sandwich and a bowl of soup – and keep the old pub for when I drop down at night, on the occasions when the isolation gets to me and I need some alcohol in my bloodstream to stop me from slitting my wrists, or to give me the courage to do so. I don't buy any drink for the cottage. That's a slippery slope.

The old pub and the new pub are alike in most respects and are officially named after their owners, but everyone refers to them in this way. The old pub has been serving liquor on the island since 1873 and the current owner is the great-grandson or great-great-grandson of the original publican. The new pub, on the other hand, has only been in operation since 1956 and has changed hands several times in the intervening decades. The current proprietor is a man in his fifties who looks as if he would like to talk to me, but I make sure to carry a book to defend my privacy, and this seems to put him off. He's not unattractive, but I have not come to the island in search of romance, and I don't want to encourage him by being too friendly. There's a ring on his finger anyway. I looked, despite myself.

Of course, it's only my vanity that makes me assume he's interested in me, for I am accustomed to being admired, but then I go to the bathroom and, while washing my hands, examine my face in the mirror and continue to be surprised by the changes I see there. The brutal haircut, for one. The skin beginning to dry out now that I no longer apply a succession of daily serums and moisturizers. A decent body, yes, but it's hidden beneath my various layers. There's no particular reason why any man would look at me twice, other than out of loneliness. But, again, I'm not looking for passion from the new pub, just a sandwich and a bowl of soup.

I've only been on the island a week when I am stopped in the street by a man who introduces himself as Fr Onkin but who invites me to call him Ifechi. May God forgive me, but the first thing I think when I see him is that this man is as black as the ace of spades, a phrase my mother always used but which I have more sense than to say aloud now. He's no islander, that's for sure, but he has a smile that warms me and the most perfect set of teeth I have ever seen on a man. He's young, no more than thirty, and seems genuinely pleased to make my acquaintance.

'And you're Mrs . . .' he asks, raising an eyebrow, and I almost say the name from which I have unshackled myself but catch myself in time.

'Miss Hale,' I tell him, aware how spinsterish this sounds, like a lady's companion in an E. M. Forster novel. 'But please, call me Willow.'

'What a beautiful name,' he says.

'As is yours,' I tell him. 'Ifechi. I've never heard it before.'

'It means the light of God,' he replies.

'Appropriate, then.'

'Yes, although it was not my choice, of course. My parents, naturally.'

'And, if you don't mind my asking, Ifechi,' I say, 'where do you come from?'

He tells me that he was born in Nigeria, in a place called Benin City, the traditional home of the Edo people. I don't know who the Edo people are and think that I might look them up on Wikipedia when I get back to the cottage but then remember that I have no Wi-Fi. Perhaps I will search on my phone the next time I'm in the old pub, assuming the promise of a connection there is true. Curiously, the new pub has none. Although it does have a pool table.

'You're new here,' he says, half a question, half a statement, and I admit that I am. 'We don't get many new people.'

'No, I wouldn't imagine so. I suppose everyone is gossiping about me.'

'Everyone and their mother,' he replies, then breaks into a cheerful laugh, which makes me laugh too. He is a comfortable presence and I like him. 'Will we see you on Sunday, Willow?' he asks.

'In the church? I'm afraid not, Ifechi. I'm not that way inclined.'

I don't tell him that I've met three popes.

'Of course,' he says, and, to my relief, makes no

attempt to convert me. 'But should you ever feel like a few moments of peace and quiet, the church is open throughout the day and mostly empty. It can be a good place to catch one's thoughts, away from the world. You can talk to God, talk to yourself, or talk to no one at all. If you feel so moved, you can even have a snooze in the pews.' He laughs at the rhyme but, this time, I just smile. I feel it's a rehearsed line, often repeated.

The truth is, I've never been religious, although I was brought up a Catholic, and Brendan insisted that we attend Mass every Sunday when the girls were young. I was happy enough to do so – everyone else did, after all – and stood and knelt at the right moments, shaking hands with neighbours and incanting prayers while never, for even a moment, thinking about the words. Brendan, on the other hand, liked to feel that he was not just part of the community but one of its leaders. Occasionally, he read the lesson on a Sunday, and it could be embarrassing how much effort he put into the nuance and characters of the Bible stories, adopting ridiculous voices that made the girls blush in mortification, and regularly served as a minister of the Eucharist, dispensing Holy Communion to parishioners when the church was too full for the priest to feed us all on his own.

The church, I might add, was on the grounds of Terenure College, an all-boys school that had, for generations, presented itself as a bastion of rugby and Catholicism. Brendan did not attend that school as a child, but he liked to be seen there on a Sunday morning. He was friends with the school librarian, Fr Odran Yates, and invited him over for dinner from time to time, the pair of them sitting in our good room talking about rugby and swimming and GAA as if I wasn't even present. If we'd had a son, he would doubtless have been a student, but, fortunately for the child, we did not. The school must feel a debt of gratitude to my husband. Across the last year, he has pushed it off the front pages.

Still, despite my lack of religious scruple, perhaps I will call into Ifechi's church some day. He makes it sound welcoming and it's not as if I have a busy schedule. We shall see.

'You've made quite the sacrifice,' I say before we part, and he looks at me quizzically.

'Sacrifice?' he asks. 'I don't understand.'

'Living here,' I tell him. 'In such an isolated spot. And, of course, there's the celibacy issue too. That can't be easy.' I pause. Why I'm interested in the poor man's sex life, or lack thereof, is anyone's guess. 'Forgive me,' I say. 'I don't know why I said that. It's none of my business. I've only just met you.'

'Celibacy is a curse,' he says, reaching for my hand, and I allow him to take it. His palms are soft, and, for one strange moment, I wonder how it might feel for them to move across my breasts or between my legs. 'But you must understand, there is only one thing in the world that I love more than women.'

'And what is that?' I ask.

'God.'

'But God won't keep you warm in your bed at night, will he?'

Later, when I too am alone in my single bed, I wonder whether God is looking over me and, if he is, what punishment he will send my way next. A dead daughter. A husband in jail. My family's reputation shattered. An entire country convinced that I was complicit in all of it. What more can he do to hurt me?

'Are you there, God?' I whisper into the darkness, remembering a book title from many years ago. 'It's me, Willow.'

But, of course, it's not Willow at all. I can call myself Willow Hale till the cows come home but, underneath, I'm still Vanessa Carvin. I just can't let anyone know.

3

SOON, I FIND MYSELF embroiled in an argument.

It's late morning and I'm reading one of the books I brought with me, a biography of Joan of Arc, when a loud, aggressive rapping sounds on the front door of the cottage. Before I can rise from the sofa, it's flung open, revealing a person of around sixty who, I think, might be a woman, although it's not immediately obvious. She must pay as little attention to her appearance as I do. While my decision to neglect my looks is still new, however, hers seems to have been a lifetime's work.

'There you are, you wee scut,' she barks, although she is not looking in my direction. 'I knew I'd find you here.'

'Who are you?' I say, jumping to my feet, alarmed by this extraordinary intrusion. 'What do you want?'

'I've come for bananas,' she says, turning to me now, her face red with rage. 'You've been feeding bananas, I know you have, so don't deny it.' She raises a thick finger and jabs it in the air. 'You're not here a wet weekend and you think you can just do as you like?'

I stare at her in bewilderment and glance towards the kitchen area in search of a weapon, should this belligerence turn violent. Unfortunately, there's nothing there but an empty cup and a teaspoon, neither of which seems likely to prove useful should I need to defend myself.

'I don't know what you're talking about,' I protest. 'I don't have any bananas. I don't even like bananas.'

'Bananas!' she roars, before pointing at the cat, who has risen to her feet, and appears to be considering a quick dart out the front door. 'You've been feeding Bananas!'

'Bananas is the cat?' I ask, understanding now.

'Of course Bananas is the cat! What else would Bananas be?'

'Well, I don't know her name, do I?' I say, raising my voice for the first time. 'She didn't introduce herself when she invited herself in.'

'Bananas is a tom,' she grunts, and the cat descends from his throne before strolling nonchalantly over to his mistress, delighted to be the centre of an argument between two women, thus establishing his sex beyond any doubt.

'I'm sorry,' I say, hoping to defuse the situation. 'I thought she – he – was a stray.'

'There are no strays on the island,' she says. 'Everyone and everything is accounted for.' She glances towards the kettle now. 'Well, are we having a cup of tea or not?'

I scurry over to the sink and fill the kettle, not daring to protest. The woman has already removed her coat and gloves and is settling herself into the armchair, Bananas' erstwhile retreat.

'You can't feed him,' she tells me. 'He has irritable bowel syndrome.'

'He wasn't wearing a medical bracelet,' I reply.

'Anyway, I've only given him a few bits and pieces. Some leftover chicken. A few saucers of milk.'

'And he's lactose-intolerant.'

A cat with such refined notions seems absurd to me but I choose not to argue. The sound of the water bubbling to a boil fills the room and I take down two mugs from the shelf.

'How do you like it?' I ask.

'How do I like what?'

'Your tea.'

'The way God intended. Milk and three sugars.'

I wait by the sink, deciding that when I sit, I will take my place at the table, which is a comfortable distance from this extraordinary creature. I glance over at Bananas, who is licking his testicles. How did I never notice them before? I wasn't looking, I suppose.

'Well, I'm sorry,' I say, putting a couple of tea bags into the pot and filling it with hot water. 'I didn't know. But I do now. So I'll stop.'

'He's a wee scut,' she insists. 'The lads who stayed here before you, they used to feed him too, so he marches over every morning in hope. I'd say he couldn't believe his luck when you showed up.'

'What lads?' I ask, bringing the pot over and setting it down on the table. 'I thought the cottage was empty before I arrived?'

She waves this away, her expression suggesting that she can't quite believe how stupid I am. 'It was three years ago,' she says. 'They only stayed a month. Queer fellas. We ran them.'

'Do you mean strange?' I ask, uncertain how contemporary her vocabulary might be. 'Strange in what way?'

'Strange enough,' she replies. 'Partners, as they say.' She makes inverted-comma symbols in the air and rolls her eyes. 'Did you ever hear the like?'

'Then you mean they were gay,' I tell her. 'Not queer.'

'Oh, is that what I mean, is it?'

'It is,' I tell her. She unsettles me, this woman, but I'm not willing to let her away with such language. There's a lengthy pause while she stares in my direction, getting the measure of me, I suppose, before she replies.

'Gay, then,' she concedes, and I realize that I have no reason to be frightened of her, after all. She's just a bully. And like all bullies, one only has to stand up to them and they fall like dominoes. 'One of them called himself a painter and the other said he was writing a play, but I didn't believe a word of it.'

'Why not?'

She shrugs her shoulders and mutters something that I don't catch.

'They were the last ones to stay here,' she says, clearer now. 'I don't know if Peadar told you.'

'He didn't,' I admit. 'But then, it's none of my business really, is it? Why would I care?'

'I like to know where I'm sleeping,' she says.

Now it's my turn to roll my eyes. Perhaps I'm being narrow-minded, but I suspect this woman has never slept in any bed other than her own, on this tiny island, since the day she was born.

'Right,' I say, thinking about my small bedroom and

wondering how two young men could have slept in that single bed, because it has clearly been a fixture of the cottage for many years, and not something purchased in advance of my arrival. Maybe they enjoyed the closeness of it. Maybe it made them love each other even more. In all my years of sleeping with Brendan, after a brief cuddle when the lights were turned off, we tended to keep as much space between us as possible.

'And how did you run them, if you don't mind my asking?'

'Do you have a slice of cake to go with this, no?' she asks as I pour the tea and hand her a cup.

'I don't,' I say.

'Very hospitable.'

'How did you run them?'

'A delegation showed up at their door,' she says. Now it's her turn to challenge me. She's not going to let a blow-in like me look down her nose at her. 'That door there, if you please.' She nods in the direction of the front door. 'And they were told what was what. We couldn't be having it. Not here. Not on the island.'

'Disgraceful,' I say. 'A mob bullying two young gay men away? What is this, the 1950s? Don't they have as much right to be here as anyone?'

'You make a very weak cup of tea,' she replies, ignoring my question. 'You should let it brew longer. Did your mammy never teach you that?'

'No,' I say. I want to learn more about the bullying of the two boys but find that I haven't the energy to ask any more questions. Rebecca, if she was here, would be dragging the woman out by her ears, but she's young and doesn't yet recognize that life can get in the way of principles. We grow too tired to fight. And so, I limit myself to this: 'We have a gay Taoiseach, of course. I'd imagine he'd have something to say about that sort of thing.'

'He can say what he likes, that fella,' says the woman, and I can tell that she's only a heartbeat away from spitting on the floor at the mention of his name. 'But he's never set foot here, has he? I'd say he'd have difficulty finding the island on a map. Go on so. Tell me your name. If you're going to be living here, we might as well be acquainted.'

'Are you the census taker?'

'That's a joke, is it?'

'I'm Willow Hale,' I tell her, sighing a little, exhausted by her belligerence. 'And you?'

'Mrs Duggan.'

'No first name?'

'Mrs.'

'Well, I'm pleased to meet you, Mrs Duggan. Tell me, do you always break into houses unannounced? Most people wait to be invited in.'

'Only vampires,' she says and, again, I'm surprised that she would know such a thing. Will I spend my time on this island realizing that all my presumptions about people are wrong? 'And I didn't break in, did I? Sure, didn't I see you sitting there through the window? Reading your book. You're one of those, I suppose.'

'One of what?'

'Readers.'

I don't know how to respond to this remark, which appears to be some form of accusation. I enjoy books, yes, but I'm far from a bibliophile. In Terenure, I was a member of a book club, but that was mostly because I could find no way out of it. My friends were involved, and Brendan liked the idea of the National Swimming Federation wives socializing in civilized or philanthropic ways. We ran fundraisers. Spent a night out on the streets before Christmas to support the homeless. And, yes, we read contemporary novels and sat in each other's living rooms and discussed them. It was never something I enjoyed, if I'm honest. In general, I don't like talking about books. I prefer simply to read them.

'Willow Hale,' she says when I haven't replied, mulling over my assumed identity. 'You know Nora Hale, I suppose?'

'I don't,' I tell her.

'Ah you do,' she says irritably, as if I'm just being difficult. 'Nora Hale. From Galway. You're one of her people, I'd say?'

'I'm not. I've never heard of her.'

'A nice enough woman,' she says, considering it, and I suspect this is the greatest compliment she can pay anyone. 'But her husband is the devil incarnate.'

I say nothing, even though it's obvious that she wants me to ask. But I have no interest in the misadventures of strangers' husbands. I have enough on my hands dealing with the misadventures of my own. Tired of being ignored,

Bananas, from the corner, miaows, and Mrs Duggan informs him, in no uncertain terms, that he would be well advised to hold his tongue.

'Have you come far?' I ask finally, aware that I sound like the late queen.

'From over there,' she says, nodding in some vague direction that might be anywhere.

'The farm with the cows?'

'That's the one.'

'So, we're neighbours.'

'For now.'

'What does that mean? Do you intend to run me too?'

She smiles, and to my astonishment her face lights up when she does so, and then she throws her head back in laughter. I can't help myself. I laugh too. I taste my tea and offer a further concession.

'You're right,' I admit. 'It is weak.'

'Will you be with us long?' she asks.

'I've taken the cottage on a month-by-month basis. I'll decide in time.'

'You don't have parties, do you?' she asks. 'We can't be doing with parties.'

I stare at her, wondering how she could possibly imagine that I would. Who would I invite?'

'No. No parties,' I assure her.

'Good. The queer lads had their music blaring half the night. Mr Duggan wanted to come over but was frightened of what might happen if he did, so I had to do it instead. I read them the riot act, have no fear.'

'What was he frightened of?'

'That they might try to have their way with him.'

I smother a laugh. If Mrs Duggan is anything to go by, I suspect that her husband would be of no interest to either of them, whose side I have taken in this historic row.

'And you'll be from Dublin, I suppose,' she continues, employing a tense that I'm not sure exists in the language.

'I am,' I say.

'What part?'

I'm surprised by the question. I can't imagine she knows Dublin at all.

'Terenure,' I say.

'The rugby players,' she replies, astonishing me even further.

'You mean the school?' I ask.

'I do. Sure, they're always winning cups, aren't they?'

'I'm surprised you'd know such a thing.'

'I read the papers,' she says, sitting up straighter now, apparently offended. 'And I'm what you might call a sports aficionado.'

She pronounces the word slowly, carefully in syllables, as if she wants me to be impressed by the extent of her vocabulary.

'It means a person who has an enthusiasm for a subject,' she clarifies.

'I know,' I say.

'We have little enough of it on the island, of course,' she says. 'A few good hurlers, I suppose. But they do say that Evan Keogh is as good a footballer as anyone has ever seen.'

'Who's Evan Keogh?'

'The Keogh lad,' she replies, which clarifies nothing. 'Charlie Keogh wants him to go off to England and get a trial with a club over there. But, from what I hear, Evan isn't keen. Charlie's a bitter piece of work, though. Wanted to be a footballer himself but wasn't good enough. Still, I'd bet everything in my pockets on him getting his way in the end. But keep that to yourself, you. I don't want him hammering on my door some evening with a flea in his ear.'

'No, I can only imagine how annoying that would be,' I say, wondering with whom I would spread such gossip, even if I was interested in it, which I'm not.

'And where, pray tell, is Mr Hale?' she asks now, raising her voice and looking around, as if a man might unexpectedly appear from the fridge or drop down from the ceiling, like Tom Cruise in that film.

'There is no Mr Hale,' I reply, which is true, for there isn't. There's a Mr Carvin, of course, but he's nearly two hundred kilometres away in Midlands Prison.

'You're not married?' she asks, raising an eyebrow in disapproval.

'I'm divorced,' I say. A lie, but near enough to the truth.

'Marriage is for life,' she tells me. 'What God joins together, may no man split asunder. You're married.'

'I'm divorced,' I insist.

'Have it your way. But you're not. We had a divorcée on the island before. She came over after her husband cheated on her and tried to get in with poor Denny Albright.'

I have no idea who poor Denny Albright is either, and don't ask.

'And what happened to her?' I ask.

'We ran her.'

It occurs to me that I was fortunate not to meet Mrs Duggan on my first day here. The warmth of her welcome might have undone me entirely.

'And you and Mr Duggan,' I say. 'How long have you been married?'

'Forty-five years,' she tells me. 'We got married on my sixteenth birthday.'

'That's very young,' I reply. 'How old was he?'

'Thirty-one.'

There's so much I'd like to say, so much I'd like to know, but, like Bananas, I understand that it's best to remain silent.

'Do you have children?' I ask.

'Of course we do,' she snaps, as if even the question is ridiculous. 'Eight. Four of each. They're all away now, save Luke. We keep him here to help out on the farm.'

'I think I've seen him,' I say, for, on my perambulations, I've been vaguely aware of a figure in the distance, calling out to the cows and herding them around the fields. It disturbs me to hear her speak of the boy as if he's a possession. Doesn't she know that you should love your child, want to spend every moment with them, because you never know when they'll be taken from you?

'Don't get any ideas about Luke,' she says, glowering at me now. 'He's a good boy and we'd like to keep him that way.'

'I'll do my best,' I say.

'Do more than your best.'

The tea has turned cold now, and I hope that she'll stand up and leave, taking the troublesome cat with her, but she shows no desire to go. Instead, she asks the question that I knew was coming next. The one I had hoped to avoid.

'And you?' she asks. 'Do you have any children yourself?'

4

I WAS NEVER WHAT you might call a natural mother, but I loved my daughters and did everything I could to ensure that they enjoyed a happy and secure childhood. My own had been untroubled and, having come through it without any noticeable scars, I simply emulated my own mother's behaviour. Businesslike and efficient, without being overly sugary.

I am, I suppose, part of that last generation of Irish women who did not recognize that they had the right to a career outside the home, and the courage to demand one. I just took it for granted that, one day, I would meet a suitable man, marry, bear children, and live a standard middle-class existence. I didn't expect or ask for more.

When Brendan and I married, he was keen to start a family immediately, but, as I hoped to wait a few years, I made the mistake of suggesting that we use the condoms that were finally accessible in Ireland. Too embarrassed to go into a chemist's and ask for them from a judgemental pharmacist, I had made my way into Trinity College, where I'd half-heartedly completed an undergraduate degree in English Literature a few years earlier, and where enthusiastic, priapic students handed them out free of charge to all and sundry from large plastic tubs, a kick to the governments and clergy that had controlled the state for so long. There was something erotic about accepting a handful of prophylactics from a handsome, grinning boy only a few years younger than me, who smiled as if to say, *You're doing it, then? So am I! We could do it together, if you like?*, but when I presented a trio of foil-encased liberators to Brendan, he looked at me as if I was the Whore of Babylon and insisted that I throw them away.

'What did we get married for if not to have children?' he asked, and I couldn't think of a good answer to his question, which is to neither his nor my credit. So we went about things in the usual way, five or six nights out of seven, but, try as we might, no baby was conceived.

Despite his old-fashioned tendencies, I was happy with Brendan during those early years. His unconscious disdain for women seemed no different to that of most Irish men, although not, perhaps, the sensual boy who had given me the johnnies under the shade of Front Arch, his fingers stroking my palm as he did so, and whose face, for some inexplicable reason, remained in my mind for years afterwards, occasionally supplanting Brendan's at the moment of climax. No, that boy looked like he loved, adored and worshipped women. As if he couldn't get enough of us. But, a decade older than me, Brendan was more attuned with the previous generation than his and didn't care for the tide of change that was decanting across the land. He would switch channels whenever President Robinson appeared on the news; her voice, he claimed, gave him a headache. He had an inexplicable hatred for Hillary Clinton, who had only recently risen to prominence. And while he addressed all the boys who were making their way through the junior ranks of the National Swimming Federation by name, those lacking in a penis were simply called 'The Girls', a homogeneous and indivisible collective.

As head of that organization, at a time when swimming was becoming a more high-profile sport in Ireland, Brendan thrived on his minor celebrity status, embracing every opportunity to appear before a camera or microphone. He was a regular contributor to radio programmes and, once in a while, would be invited as a guest on *The Late Late Show*, where I would sit in the audience and play the part of dutiful wife. Perhaps it was his growing arrogance that proved the reason why he was loath to confide in a doctor our failure to conceive, particularly when the doctor in question was a woman.

Her name was Dr Jennifer Soren, and, at our first meeting, she asked what I assume was a perfectly standard set of questions about our sex life. Naturally, I felt a little awkward answering them, but I recognized their necessity. Brendan, however, found them intrusive and when she asked whether I had been sexually active before meeting my husband, he practically leapt from his chair in outrage. This, in fact, had long been a bone of contention between us for, when we were dating, we had revealed our sexual history to each other, and it turned out that while I had had three previous lovers, two of whom had been one-night stands, Brendan was still a virgin. Although this might seem a little bizarre for a thirty-four-year-old man, in 1995 Ireland it was not quite as eccentric or worrisome as it would be today. And I rather liked the fact that he was an innocent. It suggested to me, wrongly, that he respected women and did not see us as creatures who existed purely to satisfy his needs.

The truth was that his parents had instilled a fear of sexuality in him from an early age, convincing him that he should be ashamed of his natural desires. I never knew them well – within five years of my meeting Brendan, they were both dead – but I always felt they believed there was something distasteful about their son having a girlfriend at all, let alone a wife. The day he moved out of their home, which coincided with our return from our honeymoon, was an exercise in mortification, his mother crying at the kitchen table and his father despairing over who was going to cut the grass from now on.

Repression was their legacy to their son, who struggled with my inconsequential sexual history, and I teased him about being so conventional until I recognized that he did not appreciate the joke. It was a subject that soon became out of bounds for us, but, when we argued, he could always be relied upon to suggest that he should be congratulated for taking me as his wife when other men would have walked away. The implication, of course, being that I was a slut. But, in the minds of men like Brendan, all women are sluts and are to be treated as such. The words might have changed over the years, each one replaced by something more toxic and violent, but there is always one in common parlance, mostly uttered by men, but sometimes by handmaiden women, each one designed to make us understand how deeply men's desire for us makes them hate us even more.

Things grew more difficult when, having conducted a series of tests and found nothing amiss, Dr Soren invited Brendan to produce a sperm sample for analysis. He was enraged by the suggestion that our inability to conceive could have anything to do with him and, at first, refused, which led to the first great argument of our marriage.

'I think you've been dishonest with me,' he said as we sat at home, Brendan fuming at the indignity of being asked to masturbate into a cup, especially as he knew that he would ultimately have no choice but to submit to the doctor's request if we were ever to have a baby.

'In what way?' I asked.

'I need you to tell me the truth, Vanessa,' he said. 'Those fellas you were with before me. Did you get pregnant by one of them, is that it? Did you go across the water?'

'You can't possibly imagine that I would keep something like that a secret from you,' I said.

'Well, what else am I to think?' he roared. 'I've read about it. Women who don't keep themselves tidy, then take the boat to Liverpool to have the baby sucked out of them, and then they can't get pregnant afterwards. Sure, their insides are all destroyed.'

'Dr Soren has already said that there's nothing wrong with my "insides", as you put it,' I replied, trying to control my temper. 'I've never been pregnant, I've never had an abortion, but if I had, I would have told you, and I wouldn't be ashamed of it.'

'That doesn't surprise me,' he said. 'Sure you had no shame about riding those other lads before me, did you?'

'Not a bit,' I said, wanting to hurt him now, just as he was hurting me. 'You're just jealous, that's all, that you didn't get your share when you were younger. I'm surprised you're so offended at the idea of wanking into a cup; you must have spent years playing with yourself in your mammy's upstairs room.'

He didn't like that one bit, but it was the truth, I knew it was. We didn't speak for days afterwards, and something shifted in our relationship then. Eventually, however, fuming and discomfited, he submitted to Dr Soren's requests. And, as it turned out, there was nothing wrong with him either. We were just being unlucky. The only advice she could give us was to keep trying, which we did, and then, in time, I fell pregnant with Emma.

I should add that unpleasant moments like this were the exception between us and not the rule. For the most part, Brendan was a kind and attentive husband, the sort of man who might surprise me with an unexpected dinner out or a weekend away. He chose birthday and Christmas presents with care – I never woke up to a food blender, unwrapped and still in the Arnott's bag, with the receipt languishing at the base – and kept himself fit and well groomed, as much for my sake as his own. He only unearthed his nasty side whenever his fragile masculinity was brought into question. And I loved him, I truly did. Although, of course, as it turned out, I barely knew him at all.

Emma was the most uncomplicated baby a first-time

mother could wish for. She slept well, ate whatever was put in front of her, and seemed endlessly fascinated by the world around her. I suffered no post-natal depression and grew sceptical over the horror stories I'd heard about how difficult motherhood could be. When I took her for walks in her pram, other women stopped to comment on how beautiful she was and, as if she was aware of the compliments coming her way, she would smile and extend her arms towards them. Maybe she was trying to get away from me.

To my surprise, however, Brendan, the prime mover in our decision to become parents, was not as attentive a father as I had expected. He was disappointed not to have had a son and made no attempt to hide this. It wasn't unusual that he didn't change nappies or do any of the feeds, most men didn't in those days, so that didn't bother me, but I was baffled by his indifference towards the baby. Whatever disappointment I felt, however, was more than compensated for by the bond I was building with my daughter and, after a year passed, it was I who suggested that we have another child in order that Emma would not grow up without a playmate.

'We'll try for a boy this time,' was his response, as if either of us had any say over the outcome. And, a year later, Rebecca was born.

The opposite of her sister in almost every respect, Rebecca was problematic from the moment of conception. My pregnancy left me feeling enfeebled and bilious, and while Emma had popped painlessly out of me, as if she simply wanted to get going on life without another moment's delay, Rebecca's was a long and challenging labour that required the intervention of two doctors and a fleet of nurses. When she finally appeared in a tsunami of blood, shit and screaming, Brendan looked like he was going to throw up with the drama of it all, and when he saw that I'd been delivered of a girl, he muttered, 'Ah Christ!' under his breath, loud enough for those in the room to exchange looks that suggested this would be the talk of the tea-room later.

When we brought her home, she was impossible. She would only sleep when I was awake but insisted on attention when I could scarcely keep my eyes open. She refused most foods but demanded to sample everything that came into her orbit before scrunching her face up in indignation as the flavours hit her taste buds, before spitting them back at me. She would scream for no reason, earth-shattering sounds that bore into my skull and made me feel that I was going mad. She hated being bathed and this nightly ritual soon became so traumatic that I assigned the job to Brendan, refusing to have anything more to do with it.

'Sure what do I know about washing a baby?' he asked, as if I was asking him to scale Mount Kilimanjaro or paint an Old Master.

'You know how to wash yourself, don't you?' I shouted at him, unable to put up with his indolence any longer. 'It's no different. There's just less of her.'

The only thing, or rather the only person, who could soothe Rebecca was Emma, who would toddle over to her sister as she lay screaming on her mat and collapse next to her, placing a small hand upon her forehead, and, in that instant, she would calm down. Although they were different in so many ways, there was an extraordinary connection between them from the start and I was grateful that Emma did not show any signs of jealousy. She had a way with Rebecca that both Brendan and I lacked. Or maybe Rebecca simply preferred her to us.

Was I as insentient to Emma's needs even then? Was I a terrible mother from the start, driven, as I was, by status and my busy social life, viewing her as just another accessory, like my necklaces or earrings or perfumes? If I dwell on these questions too much, I will bang my head against the wall until I, like her, am dead. I failed her. And yet they are ever-present, fighting to be answered, challenging me constantly.

That sisterly bond was to grow and strengthen in the years that followed, and while they say that a parent never gets over the death of a child, I think it is Rebecca who will suffer the most in the decades to come. Emma, only two years older, was the mother she needed, and she can't forgive me her loss. It's an injustice, but I suspect she blames me more than Brendan for what happened.

The next few years were so taut that there was no more talk of babies after that, until both girls had started school, when I experienced an unexpected rush of loneliness and decided that I might like one more.

I suggested as much to Brendan, but he refused even to countenance the idea. (By now, he had decided that condoms were not such a terrible idea after all, and our sex life, while hardly as busy as it had once been, had not entirely vanished.)

'I'm surrounded by women as it is,' he said, trying to make a joke of it. 'I'm not going to be outnumbered even more.'

'But we might have a boy this time,' I protested, but he wouldn't be convinced, and, in time, I made my peace with it. A family of four, after all, was more than many had. Not quite a Gentleman's Family, but close enough.

Still, I've always felt certain that we were supposed to have a third child, and that if we had, it would have been a boy. I'm so convinced of this that I occasionally find myself mourning the son that I did not have as much as the daughter that I did.

I would have called my son Zac, a name I have always loved, but in our family, he would have been called Zaccy, until puberty hit, when he would have demanded that we revert to his given name. And, although he would have been the youngest, I believe this ghost-child would have protected us all.

5

I TAKE IFECHI'S ADVICE and decide to make a pilgrimage to the church, standing outside for a long time before deciding whether to enter. If there is a God, I want to make it clear to Him that I'm not here for spiritual reasons, but simply to understand the island better. It's a small stone building, the right size, I suppose, for such a tiny population, and, unlike the much grander one I attended throughout my married life, it has a humility to it. The front doors are open but, from where I stand, with the sun shining before me, I can see nothing but darkness ahead. Still, something summons me inside.

It takes a few moments for my eyes to adjust to the interior gloom and I instinctively reach out to dip my index finger into the holy-water font before touching it to my forehead. It was hot outside but it's cool in here. On a cold day, I imagine those conditions are reversed, as if the church is a place of opposites. I remain at the back for a few moments, my attention taken by a wire rack holding a collection of information booklets that look as if they're even older than the building itself. I notice the familiar figure of Padre Pio, his hands joined in prayer, on the cover of one; the Virgin Mary, her arms outstretched in supplication, on another. Beneath my feet, the ground is tiled with what appears to be a granite mosaic, sprinkled with an occasional floral design.

There are few people present. A man seated at the end of the second pew, hunched over with his head in his hands. A woman, six rows behind him, on her knees and clicking a set of rosary beads between her fingers as her lips move soundlessly. Most surprising of all is the sight of a teenage boy seated only a few feet from where I stand, next to the confession box. I glance in his direction and, at the same moment, a light flicks on above the box and the boy stands, opens the door and makes his way inside. He can't be more than seventeen and not only does it surprise me that he would have sins to confess, but, if he does, that he would have any interest in doing so.

Churchgoing, as I have mentioned, was more Brendan's area than mine, because Fr Yates' friendship mattered to him, and the parishioners' recognition of him strengthened his belief in his own importance. What he never understood, however, is that religion begins in the soul, not the ego.

I'm drawn to the Stations of the Cross, seven hanging on one wall, and seven on the other. I've always been intrigued by these, for an artistic priest can use a little imagination in the commissioning of a design as there seems to be no demands on their style and they differ from church to church. Here hangs a set of fabrics, painted in black ink upon a linen background, that recall the work of Japanese calligraphers. They are very beautiful. As I cross the nave to the right-hand side and examine the tenth station, *Jesus is Stripped of His Garments*, I am struck by the expression the artist has imposed upon His face, blending confusion, dismay and humiliation. For once, the Son of God appears almost human.

The whole business of the Twelve Apostles has always bothered me, the hard-nosed maleness of their clique, the decision from the start to exclude women from their number. Most became saints, I think, but did that prevent them from leering at the women who served their food, or making vulgar remarks about girls they noticed on the streets? Did James lose interest during the Sermon on the Mount, his attention captured by the breasts of a young woman seated near him? Did John lure a serving girl at the Wedding at Cana into an anteroom and press himself against her, ignoring her pleas to be released? And what of Andrew, or Matthew, or Judas Iscariot? Did they take women without permission, forcing their unwashed parts into unwilling bodies whenever they felt so moved? All these men, all these fucking men. Sacred and hallowed and venerated for two thousand years. And yet it was the women, and only the women, who were there for Him at the end when the men betrayed Him, denied Him, ran from Him, pocketed their thirty pieces of silver for traducing Him. Here is Veronica wiping His face. Here are the women of Jerusalem greeting Him as He carries His burden. Here is Mary, weeping at the base of the cross. Loyal women; unfaithful and treacherous men. The former left to gather up His soiled and bloody clothes; the latter sanctified.

Oh, I feel such anger.

It's now that my mind turns to Gareth Wilson and Niamh Loomis.

Gareth, that formidable man, six foot four in height and built of pure iron, standing in the dock of the Four Courts in Dublin, focused entirely on salvaging his reputation as he spoke of the man he personally installed as Director of the National Swimming Federation, and by whose side he stood for years. Swearing that he knew nothing of my husband's behaviour and can still hardly believe it, for a more dedicated servant of the sport he cannot imagine. And then Niamh, his secretary of fifteen years, being questioned by Brendan's barrister, who feigned disbelief that such crimes could have taken place without her noticing any of it.

'You never had any children yourself, Miss Loomis, did you?' he asked, as if this had any relevance to the matter at hand. 'Or married, for that matter. Was there a reason for that?'

Objections raised, the question left unanswered, but the implication of her nature left to settle in the minds of the jury. It is imperative to find a woman to blame for a man's crimes.

Then my own interrogation, of course, the questions approved by my husband, where the culpability was extended to me.

Did you love your husband, Mrs Carvin?

Did you have a natural sexual relationship with your husband, Mrs Carvin?

Were you ever unfaithful to your husband, Mrs Carvin?

You struggled to conceive your first child, didn't you, Mrs Carvin?

Were you affectionate with your husband, Mrs Carvin, or could you be, shall we say, prone to mood swings?

Would you call yourself a good wife, Mrs Carvin?

From above, the chorus of hissing from a group of mothers who would have tumbled into the dock to tear my husband limb from limb if they could, turning their fury on anyone who tried to stop them, their teeth bared, their fingers curled like claws.

Next to me during all these testimonies sat Rebecca, her body rigid, her face set like stone, grinding her teeth in so annoying a fashion that I wanted to slap her.

And finally, after his conviction, after his sentencing and his disgrace, the pundit who wrote in his newspaper column that while his actions should be condemned, no one should forget just how much Brendan Carvin had done for Irish sport and that, in the end, we should be grateful for that at least. Outrage, of course. Social media up in arms. The usual half-hearted apology – *if I offended anyone* – but he meant what he had written.

The sound of someone releasing a cry of pain drags me from my reminiscences and I look ahead and realize that the man at the end of the second pew is Tim Devlin, proprietor of the new pub, the man who always seems inclined to talk to me when he brings me my sandwich and bowl of soup, and whose eye I deliberately avoid so as not to give him false hope. His right hand has transformed into a fist and he is lifting and dropping it on to his knee with metronomic insistence. This is a man in pain. This is a man with something on his conscience. The church turns claustrophobic, and I move away from the Stations, making my way back along the nave towards the doors. As I do so, I notice the teenage boy once again, for he has emerged from the confessional now, and is on his knees, his eyes closed, muttering his penance. I wonder what his friends would say if they could see him. They would mock him, I expect, but I find myself moved by such piety, which is rare in the young. It's rare in the old too, for that matter.

Outside, emerging into the sunlight, I inhale deeply, filling my lungs with air, and feel a sense of relief to have escaped a building that exists solely to comfort the troubled. There is birdsong in the air and a playful scurrying somewhere in the grass beneath me, which needs cutting but, in its unshorn state, provides a useful hiding place for unseen life. I sit down on a bench and am enjoying the feeling of the sunshine on my face when Fr Onkin appears from the church and strolls towards me, smiling, as ever.

'Good morning, Willow,' he says, opening his arms wide, displaying the palms of his hands. 'You changed your mind, I see.'

'Think of me as a tourist, Ifechi,' I say, nodding towards the space next to me and inviting him to sit down. 'I'm only here to gawk at the splendour of the place and see if I can grab the smell of incense.'

'You are nothing as transitory as a tourist,' he says, settling himself beside me. 'I think there is much more to you than that.'

'That's only because you don't know me. Inside, I'm completely empty.'

He shakes his head. He's not going to argue with me.

'Has it ever occurred to you,' I ask after an awkward silence, 'that faith is little more than a matter of geography?'

'In what way?' he asks.

'Well, think about it,' I say. 'Ireland has long been a Catholic country. Almost everybody born here was christened Catholic but had no say in the matter. Some take to it like a duck to water and build their lives around it. Others wear it as a winter coat. Then there are those who have no interest in it whatsoever but still send their children to make their First Holy Communion or their Confirmation. But if they'd been born in Israel, say, or Tehran, or Moscow, they never would have been Catholic to begin with, would they? Even the Pope, and all his predecessors, are only Catholics because of where they came from. All those Italians for so many centuries. Would any of them have discovered Catholicism if they'd been brought up in Tokyo?'

'Some, perhaps,' he says. 'Faith has a way of finding you.'

'And what about you?' I ask. 'Were you born into it?'

'In my country,' he says, 'there are two tribes. Muslims in the north, some Sunni, some Shia, and Christians in the south. But most of those Christians are Protestant, not Catholic. Maybe only one in five people in Nigeria consider themselves Catholic. I myself was brought up Protestant.'

'Really?' I say, surprised. 'So what made you defect, if that's the right word?'

He turns his face towards the bright blue sky above us, or perhaps towards heaven, and smiles. I understand. He's not going to tell me. He too has secrets.

From the door of the church, the teenage boy emerges, pulling a cheap pair of sunglasses from the open neck of his T-shirt. He's taller than I realized, and very good-looking, with an athletic build, blond curly hair and smooth skin. He glances in our direction and raises a hand to Ifechi, who nods back as the boy pulls his back-pack on and continues on his way.

'That can't be very common,' I say.

'And what is that?' he asks.

'A boy his age. Going to confession.'

He says nothing. Although I witnessed it with my own eyes, the boy's business inside the church is not something he can discuss with me.

'It is true,' he says, after much thought, 'that I do not see as many youthful faces in my congregation on a Sunday as I would wish. But there are some. That boy, Evan, is one.'

'Brought by his parents, I suppose.'

'Some are interested, even if they would never dare to admit it.'

'When I was his age, we all had to go,' I tell him. 'It would have been unheard of not to. And I brought my own children too, even though I'm not a believer. So I suppose that makes me just as big a hypocrite.'

'But something must have made you bring them,' he

insists. 'Perhaps some part of you was hoping to receive the Spirit, even if you didn't realize it?'

'I brought them to keep my husband happy,' I tell him. 'I don't know how much you know about Irish women, Ifechi, but that's what we do. It's what we've been doing for centuries now, and look where it's got us.'

'And where is that?'

'Here. To some godforsaken island in the Atlantic Ocean, where we know no one and no one knows us.'

'This island is not godforsaken,' he tells me quietly, placing a hand gently atop my own. 'No place is.'

'It was a turn of phrase, that's all,' I tell him, for I don't want to offend the man, who seems kind and devoted to his calling. Although, God knows, I'm no judge of character. 'I'm sure you bring a lot of support to your congregation.'

Another exit from the church. This time, it's the publican. He's walking quickly, his head bowed, unsettled by whatever interactions inside he had with the Lord. He doesn't look in our direction but makes his way towards the gate before turning left, in the direction of his place of business.

'Is he all right?' I ask, and Ifechi raises an eyebrow.

'In what sense?'

'He seemed upset. I saw him banging his fist against his leg.'

'Mr Devlin has been through much trauma,' he tells me.

'Has he indeed?' I ask, intrigued now. I'm not a gossip, I never have been, not even when I lived in Terenure and counted the other mothers in the parish among my friends. But life moves slowly on the island and a little bit of scandal would liven things up. As long as it's not my scandal, that is.

'Oh yes,' replied Ifechi quietly, but I can tell from his tone that he's not going to elaborate. I don't ask anything further. It would be beneath me even to try.

'Well, Ifechi,' I say, rising to my feet now. 'I should be on my way.'

'Will I see you here again, Willow?' he asks, and I think about it.

'It's not impossible.'

'If you ever want to talk, you can always knock on my door, and I will be happy to converse.'

'Thank you . . . Father,' I say, employing his correct title for the first time. He is a man worthy of my respect.

'Whatever has brought you here will one day be little more than a memory. Trust in the Lord, Willow. He trusts in you.'

I shake my head, disappointed that he would end our conversation in such a way. 'I'd never trust a man again, Ifechi,' I tell him, reverting to his given name. 'I'm not that stupid.'

6

I WAKE IN THE night to what sounds like a large animal scrambling across the roof of the cottage. It is as dark as night gets here, which is a darkness I have never known before, and, nervous for what might be lurking outside, I turn on my bedside lamp and glance at the clock, which reads 2.35 a.m. I lie very still, hoping the noise was simply an intruder in a dream, but no, there it is again, and I have no choice but to get up and investigate.

I have felt no fear since arriving on the island, even here in the comparative isolation of the cottage, but then I've never been the type to scare easily. However, I can feel my heart beating faster inside my chest as my anxiety levels rise. It crosses my mind that, should something untoward occur, a community like this would most likely stand together to protect one of its own against any accusations levelled by an outsider.

But my mind is moving too fast towards a calamitous conclusion, and I tell myself to remain composed, that it was probably nothing more than some nocturnal animal on night patrol. I pull on a heavy jumper over my night-dress, slide my feet into my slippers and step into the cold living room, standing silently in the centre, listening, waiting.

All seems quiet now, but it is not a natural silence. It is the sound of someone trying not to make a sound, a phrase I read in a novel once and that stayed with me. I reach for my phone, which is charging in the socket by the wall, and press the home button. The screensaver is a picture of Emma and Rebecca taken on that last holiday in Wexford, the day before Emma died. They have their arms around each other, and both are smiling, wearing sunglasses because it was a fine summer's day. I don't quite know why I'm bothering – is it simply for the reassurance of seeing their faces? – for who can I call? There isn't a police station on the island. Should a crime occur, a Garda is apparently despatched from Galway to make the necessary investigations. Still, it's in my hands now, so I open the messaging app and look at my most recent text to my surviving daughter. She's unblocked me once again and changed her picture. I press the required button to allow the image to fill the screen, then I save it to my photos. It was taken in a pub and Rebecca is sticking her tongue out flirtatiously at the photographer. The surroundings are familiar to me, but it's not Terenure. Somewhere in the city centre, I think. Is it Neary's? I think it might be. But who took the picture? Her expression suggests a certain intimacy so it's probably a boy. She'll be asleep now, I assume, so it should be safe to message without suffering the indignity of being immediately blocked.

If I'm still here in Winter, I type. *I think it will be hard to tell day from night.*

The message sends, a single grey tick appears. I watch it for a moment, just in case it doubles, then turns blue, but no.

Returning the phone to its charger, I move towards the front door, opening it cautiously and looking outside. It is a fine night, not a breeze in the air, and a waxing moon offers little illumination to the sweep of fields that stretch down towards the sea. I remember when one of our book club insisted on our reading *The Hours* and I could not face it, even though it was short, so watched the film instead, and then read a little about Virginia Woolf online before our meeting, desperate to have something intelligent to say. I spoke about how she filled her pockets with stones before walking into the river, all her cares scattered behind her like confetti on the riverbank. Would I be missed if, tonight, I followed her example? Would I even be found? I read that it took three weeks for the poor woman's body to be discovered, and who knows what terrible condition it was in by then. I'd prefer mine to float away and offer sustenance to the creatures of the sea, my flesh becoming one with theirs as my bones sank to the ocean floor, settling peacefully into the sand to rest there for eternity.

When Emma's body was retrieved from the beach near Curracloe, she was taken to the mortuary at Wexford General Hospital, where Brendan and I identified her together. He broke down when the sheet was lowered to reveal her face, but I found myself unable to cry. It didn't seem real to me at the time. After only twelve hours in the water, her features hadn't grown bloated, but still, the body that lay before me did not seem like that of my daughter but rather like a poor approximation of her. Something one might see at a waxworks. The attendant asked whether this was, in fact, Emma, and I said, 'I think so,' an answer that did not satisfy him, and so he turned to Brendan, who was less equivocal in his response. And then she was covered once again, and we were led from the room. All the time, I felt as if I was in a television show, or a film; it seemed impossible that such a thing could happen in real life.

I step a few feet away from the cottage now, the better to see the roof, but nothing makes its presence felt until a shape darts past my ankles and charges through the open door. I'm too surprised to scream, and by the time my breath is recovered I see that it is only Bananas, out on one of his late-night hunting sessions. Relieved, and feeling a little foolish, I'm torn between reprimanding him and wanting to take him in my arms. Despite Mrs Duggan's demands that he stay away, he has continued to be a regular visitor, but I've stopped giving him food on account of the alleged irritable bowel syndrome. I continue to offer saucers of milk, though. I don't buy the lactose intolerance for even a moment. He's a cat, after all. And cats drink milk.

Something draws me down the path that leads to the sea and I make my way along, guided by the moon and the glistening light that dances on the waves like sparks from a flint. It takes no more than ten minutes to reach the beach. I stroll along it most afternoons and could find my way there with my eyes closed. The small groups of teenagers who live on the island generally cavort around it with a mixture of excitement and tentativeness. Now that the weather is improving, the boys peacock with their shirts off, displaying scrawny chests and thin legs, while the girls tease them by removing their clothes beneath towels before magically reappearing a few moments later in two-piece swimsuits. In the sea, the young people behave chaotically, unable to control their desires and frustrations. They are masters of all they survey here, but I wonder how they will survive when adulthood takes them to Dublin, London, or further afield. They are water babies, nourished by the waves, and they will struggle when they are, by necessity, dragged to dry land.

It was through swimming, of course, that Brendan and I met, when I was twenty-one and he a decade older. I had a trip planned to Greece with two friends, to the island of Kos, and, embarrassed that I had never learned, I signed up for an intensive course of sessions in my local pool, where Brendan was assigned to be my coach. I had expected a woman to teach me and felt slightly unnerved when this tall, good-looking man approached in shorts and T-shirt, with bare legs and feet, to introduce himself. Naturally I was in my swimsuit at the time, which felt like a strange way to encounter a man for the first time. I was glad when he invited me to descend the ladder into the water, for although I was confident that I had a decent body, it was unsettling to stand in such near-nakedness before him.

He was a good teacher, calm, patient and deliberate, and it only took about six classes before my confidence grew. His too, I suppose, because he invited me out for a drink then and, having developed a crush on him, I said yes. It was so strange to go out on that first date, when both of us were fully dressed for the first time, my hair combed and not hidden beneath a cap. Goggle-less. There was a curious sensuality to it; the opposite experience of most couples who, over time, move from clothed towards a state of undress.

I didn't keep up the swimming after we were married, only starting again when Emma was a baby, when I took to driving to Dún Laoghaire after lunch every day and taking a dip in the Forty Foot. You could always rely on two or three other young mothers with children to be there and we would entrust our offspring to each other as we dived into the icy water and felt the good of it on our skin. Part of the fun was the fury on the faces of the men, who still resented the presence of women in this once sacrosanct area. Some even continued the ancient practice of swimming naked in the hope that this would intimidate us into leaving them in peace, but it would have taken more than a bunch of fat sixty-year-olds with flabby bellies drooping over sagging cocks to frighten us away.

When he learned of these afternoon trips, Brendan accused me of keeping this from him, and he wasn't entirely wrong. I wanted something for myself, even if it did echo his activities as he ascended the ranks of the National Swimming Federation. He was one of those who believed that women had no business being at the Forty Foot and, when he asked me whether there were naked men there, I said there were, on occasion, and he went into one of his moods and wouldn't come out of it for days.

Unwilling to argue, I asked would he prefer that I didn't go there any more, and he said he would, sure wasn't there a perfectly good swimming pool in Terenure College and it had a ladies' morning every Wednesday and Friday, when both Emma and I could get into the pool together.

And to keep the peace, I did as he asked. I never returned to the Forty Foot, nor did I ever again meet the friends I had inadvertently made.

On the beach now, I remove my slippers and my toes burrow into the cold, moist sand. It has none of the pleasing, warm sensation I am accustomed to from daytime, so I step forward into the water itself, intending only to wet my ankles, then feel the tide hurl itself against me in a fury, surprised and enraged by my intrusion. It dampens the base of my nightdress as if to say, *Away you, away!* It is cold. Oh, it is so cold. Was it as cold as this when you walked into the sea in Wexford, Emma? Did you plunge down into the water to break the shock of it, or did you step gingerly forward, one eye on the horizon, uncertain whether you really meant what you were doing? And how far out were you when you knew that there was no way back, even for a strong swimmer like you? In that moment, did you feel panic? Regret? Fury? Relief? I have so many questions for you, my darling girl, but you aren't here to answer them.

I recall Rebecca's question of me, after it all came out.

Did you know all along and just didn't care?

I plunge down into the water now, submerging myself up to my neck, and when my body has adjusted to the temperature, I sink lower again, beneath the waterline.

Immediately, the sounds change. It's a different universe under here. A song from an old Disney movie that the girls watched hundreds of times when they were children forms in my head and I open my eyes, looking for friendly lobsters and dancing prawns. But I am alone down here, except for the microscopic life forms moving around me, each one wondering why this interloper has disturbed their agreeable night. I don't feel cold any more but know that when I raise my head into the world again, I will. I anticipate this with regret, even anger. I would rather stay down here, like Emma did, and, tomorrow, float in on the tide.

Water has been the undoing of me. It has been the undoing of my family. We swim in it in the womb. We are composed of it. We drink it. We are drawn to it throughout our lives, more than mountains, deserts, or canyons. But it is terrible. Water kills.

I can't stay down here any longer. With no stones in my pockets, my body forces me back to the surface, and I emerge, gasping. Instinctively, I put my hands to my forehead to brush the hair out of my eyes but, of course, it is gone, scalped close, not daring to grow back in case it provokes me to get the scissors out again.

I drag myself back towards the beach, weighed down by the sodden nightdress and the woollen jumper, and look up towards the sky, feeling strangely calm now, before making my way back towards the path that leads me home, if home it is.

And it is then that I feel eyes on me, like a torch pointed towards my heart. Turning my head in the direction of the

Duggan farm, what light the moon offers reveals a figure in the distance, observing me. I cannot make out his face – he might be a scarecrow for all the movement he is making – but there is a moment of connection, where we are the only two people in the world. I pull off my jumper, for it is too heavy, the saturated wool weighing me down, and then, in an act of defiance, I slip out of the wet nightdress too and march naked towards my door. Why shouldn't I, after all? It is my door. It is my body.

Watch me all you like, Luke Duggan, if it makes you happy.

Back inside, I feel in desperate need of a hot bath and a cup of tea.

Bananas has left me a gift by the kitchen table, but what use have I of a dead mouse is a mystery to me.

Later, when sleep returns, I dream of the boy on the hill, but this time he is not just standing there watching, he is making his way down towards the sea too, only it is a different sea, an unfamiliar one, and he is throwing himself into the waves with the grace of an Olympian. He vanishes from sight for a moment, and when he emerges, he draws the air back into his empty lungs, but he is not empty-handed. No, he has found my daughter.

He is holding Emma in his arms.

He is carrying her back to the shore, back to safety, back to me.

7

WHEN HE KNOCKS ON my door a few days later, I realize that I've been expecting him to call. At first, I don't even know for sure that it is him, but the embarrassed look on his face, not to mention the vague resemblance to his mother, gives the game away. He's tall, with sandy hair that falls over his eyes, which I notice are two different colours, one pale blue, the other green. He's in his late twenties, I'd imagine, and carrying a not unpleasant musk of sweat about him.

'I'm sorry to bother you,' he says, unable or unwilling to look me in the eye. 'I'm Luke. I live in the—'

'The farm over there,' I say, nodding in the direction of his family's land. 'Yes, I know.'

'I wondered if I could have a word.'

The poor boy looks so mortified that I step out of the way and invite him in. Bananas glances up from the armchair, perhaps surprised to see a familiar face here, and jumps down on to the floor in deference.

'You may as well take it,' I say, pointing towards the vacated seat. 'He doesn't do that for just anyone. Will you have a cup of tea?'

'I won't,' he says. 'I'll not stay long.' He sits. 'Only I wanted to apologize to you.'

'Oh yes?' I ask, taking my usual spot on the sofa. 'For what?'

'A couple of nights back, I was . . . well, I was outside late. Just having a smoke above. And I saw you coming back from the beach. I didn't mean to see you, but I think you noticed me up there. It might have seemed like I was watching you, but I wasn't spying or anything like that. I'm not some . . .' He searches for the right word. 'I'm not one of those types, do you know? Who'd be out in the middle of the night looking at women in that way.'

'It's fine,' I say, not wanting him to feel any more tortured than he already does. 'I'm not surprised you stared. I imagine it's not every day you see a middle-aged woman walking back to her cottage stark naked.'

'No,' he admits, blushing a little, which is when his beauty shines through. He looks up at me now and offers a half-smile.

'You must have thought me mad.'

'Sure it takes all sorts.'

'Well, I hope you enjoyed the show.'

'I've had worse nights.'

And now it's my turn to blush. We look at each other and something strange passes between us. An understanding of some sort.

'What were you doing up at that time of night anyway?' I ask, and he shrugs his shoulders.

'I might ask you the same thing.'

'I had a nightmare. And then I woke to the sound of something on my roof. It turned out to be that wee scut there,' I say, nodding towards Bananas, who has settled on the floor, preparing for one of his regular naps. It occurs to me how quickly I have adopted the language of the island, for this was exactly the way Luke's mother described the cat on our initial encounter. 'Then I was awake anyway and something drew me towards the sea.'

'It can be dangerous down there at that time of night,' Luke tells me. 'You'd want to be careful doing that sort of thing.'

'I'm a strong swimmer.'

'No matter. Water is dangerous.'

'Oh, I know that.'

'I'm not telling you what to do but you'd be well advised only to swim when there's someone else nearby.'

'Thank you,' I say. For some reason, I don't feel patronized. After all, he's lived on the island his entire life so must know the dangers of the tides better than I ever could, and his tone is not condescending. 'You're right. I'll be more careful in the future. If you won't have a cup of tea, would you take something stronger?'

He thinks about this and smiles. A boyish expression on his face.

'Sure why not,' he says. 'If you're having one.'

I stand up and make my way towards the kitchen area, where I pour two small glasses of whiskey, dropping a large ice cube into each, and hand one across. My earlier vow not to keep alcohol in the house evaporated a few weeks ago, although I've drunk very little here. But I like to know there's something on hand in case of an emergency.

'I should have introduced myself,' I say when I sit down again. 'I'm Willow. Willow Hale.'

'Mam told me,' he says. 'She came to visit you, I believe.'

'She did. She seemed put out that I'd been feeding her cat.'

'That creature is the bane of all our existences,' he says. 'She roars at it from morning till night, but she'd trade any one of us in for it.'

It doesn't surprise me to hear this. Despite her army of children, Mrs Duggan didn't strike me as the maternal type. Not that I'm one to talk.

'So, are you enjoying yourself here anyway?' he asks after an awkward silence.

'It's giving me time to think,' I say, recognizing that this is an answer to a different question entirely.

'You're from Dublin, I'm told?'

'Yes.'

'Most people leave here to go there. Not the other way around.'

'I needed a break,' I say. 'I had some family issues and—'

'No, stop,' he says, waving a hand in the air. 'It's none of my business. I wasn't prying.'

'It's fine,' I say. It's curious, but even though we've only just met, I feel as if I could trust him with the upsetting facts of my life and he would keep them to himself. I felt the same with Ifechi. Something in the insular nature of island life, perhaps. A tendency to respect the privacy of others.

'I rarely get to talk to people, other than Mam and Dad,' he tells me. 'So I'm not the best at it. Throw me out when I get boring.'

'I will, but we're not there yet. I suppose people have mentioned David Bowie to you before?'

He nods and closes his eyes for a moment so I can no longer see the different colours of his pupils. He seems embarrassed by them, when, in fact, they only add to his attractiveness.

'I don't really know the lad myself,' he tells me. 'Some of his songs, I suppose.'

'Before your time,' I tell him. 'I grew up with him. Metaphorically speaking.'

I notice a gaping hole in the right knee of his jeans and can see the dark brown skin beneath it and a sprinkling of golden hairs. It baffles me that I feel unexpected desire for this gentle young man, who can't be more than a few years older than Rebecca. And yet I do. I can't remember the last time I felt desire for anyone. When I realize that I've gone silent, I force myself back to the conversation.

'And what about you?' I ask finally.

'What about me?'

'It must have been near three o'clock in the morning when you saw me out there. What had you up at that time?'

He reaches down to stroke Bananas, who submits to his hand, purring happily.

'I'm not the best of sleepers,' he says. 'I keep what you might call odd hours.'

'In what sense?'

'The farm,' he explains. 'It's a twenty-four-seven type of job, you know? I'd been up late the night before when one of the cows was calving and then I took a nap mid-afternoon, woke in the early morning, and couldn't get back to sleep. So I went outside for a cigarette on account of Mam having a conniption fit if I smoke in the house. Anyway, I don't really follow the clock in the way other people do. I wake, I work, I sleep, and then I do it all over again. It's all the same to me.'

'Do you enjoy it?'

He frowns, as if this is something he's never considered before.

'It's what I do, I suppose,' he tells me. 'Enjoyment doesn't really come into it. Do you mind if I use your bathroom?'

I'm about to tell him where it is – not that it's too hard to find – but he's already on his feet and making his way towards it. He's been here before, then. I remain where I am while he's gone and, when he reappears, less than a minute later, he smiles and sits down again.

'This isn't your first time in the cottage,' I say.

'Oh no,' he says. 'A couple of lads had it a few years back and I used to come over at night sometimes for a game of cards and the odd drink.'

'Your mother told me about them,' I say. 'She said there was some sort of hostility towards them from the islanders.'

'It was fucking disgraceful,' he says, surprising me with the forcefulness of his response. 'Mam led the charge, no better woman. They were a nice pair, though. No harm in them at all. They might have stayed longer had they not been made to feel so unwelcome. A shameful set of circumstances.'

'I suspect the island isn't exactly running with the times,' I say.

'No.'

'Have you been to Dublin?' I ask him, a non-sequitur, but I'm running out of things to say and don't want him to leave just yet.

'I have.'

'Do you like it there?'

'"Like" would be too strong a word,' he says. 'It can be fierce noisy, for one thing. I'm not used to that. But it makes for a change, and you need that once in a while. I had a girlfriend once from Dublin. Do you know Dundrum?'

'I do.'

'Well, she lived there, near the Town Centre. I never saw a place like it. All the shops. You'd lose your mind buying things you don't need.'

'Did she work there?'

'No, she was a teacher.'

'And how did you meet?'

'She came over with a group of students in the summer months. The ones who arrive to learn the *cúpla focal*. Áine was her name.'

'That can't have been easy,' I say. 'A long-distance relationship.'

'No. It didn't work out in the end anyway. On account of that, for the most part.'

'Do you miss her?'

'I do and I don't,' he says with a sigh. 'But sure, it's five years gone now. She might be married for all I know.'

'You don't stay in touch?'

'Ah no.'

He looks around the room, and something in the nostalgic expression on his face makes me think that he might have taken Áine here when they were dating, if the cottage was empty at the time, and used it for their trysts, for I can't imagine his mother would have allowed him to use the farmhouse. He might have slept with her in my bed. The idea sends an unexpected frisson through me.

'And you,' says Luke, rousing me from my reverie. 'Are you married yourself?'

'Divorced,' I tell him.

'I'm sorry.'

'I'm not.'

'Right.'

He strokes the cat again. I wonder is this his default move when he feels uncertain in conversation. When he looks up again, he brushes the hair out of his eyes and smiles at me and I can see that he's trying not to study my body too closely but that he can't help himself. He's lonely. It's easy to see.

'And there's just you, I'm told?' I say. 'Your mother said your brothers and sisters moved away.'

'Sure, they're long gone,' he tells me. 'Four above in

Dublin, one in America, one in Canada, one in Australia. 'Twas me drew the short straw.'

'Why is that?'

'I'm the youngest.'

'And that means you have to stay?' I ask. I'm not here to reorganize his life but I wonder does he realize how ridiculous this sounds.

'Someone has to.'

'You must never see them.'

'The eldest pair I'd have difficulty picking out of a line-up.'

'It seems unfair that you're left to look after the farm, just because of when you were born.'

He nods and sighs a little before picking at the tear in his jeans. He agrees, probably, but can't see a way out of it. His mother is made of tough stuff and will still be here, I imagine, in twenty years' time. When he's finally liberated, it will be too late for him.

'I can't imagine there's much of a social life on the island,' I continue. 'For a boy your age, I mean. How old are you anyway?'

'Twenty-four,' he says. 'I'll be twenty-five in a few weeks' time.'

'Will you have a party?'

'A few drinks, maybe. In the pub.'

'The new pub or the old pub?'

'The old pub.'

'Do you know the man who runs the new pub?' I ask, recalling my visit to the church and how distraught he seemed in his pew, beating his knee with his fist.

'I do,' he says. 'Tim Devlin.'

'Do you know much about him?'

'A bit. Why, have you taken a shine to him?'

'Oh no, it's nothing like that,' I reply quickly. I don't want him to think I would be romantically interested in a man in his fifties, even though I'm of that age myself. 'It's just, I have lunch there most days and he never speaks to me. But I saw him another time, in another place, I won't say where, and he was terribly upset. I don't want to pry but—'

'He has his troubles,' says Luke, and I wait for him to expand on this and feel both disappointment and admiration that he chooses not to. 'But then, don't we all? I have them myself.' He smiles a little as he says this. Every time he smiles, I find him more beautiful. He is wasted on this lump of rock. 'But I don't have the time to indulge them.'

'Is that a good thing or a bad thing?' I ask.

'It's a terrible thing,' he says. 'My head is wrecked half the time and I can't get it cleared.'

'You must have friends?'

'A few. One or two stayed on for the same reasons as me. But most are away to the mainland.'

'You're lonely.'

He grows more serious now as he looks at me. 'This is a fierce intense conversation, Willow Hale,' he says. 'I wasn't expecting this at all. I only came over to apologize and so you'd know I wasn't a peeping Tom.' He takes a deep breath and looks me directly in the eyes now, the first time he's done this. 'And now I feel like I want to tell you all my troubles. That I could. And that you'd let me. You're not a therapist in real life, are you?'

'Real life?' I ask, frowning.

He looks around and indicates the living room around us, the cottage, the island as a whole.

'Sure this isn't real life, is it?' he says. 'You're escaping that for your own reasons, I'm sure. I would too, but I don't know how.'

He looks down at the floor again and I feel great sympathy for him. I reach out, seeking his hand, and he takes it. His skin is rough and masculine. When we release each other, we both finish what's left in our glasses and stand. To my surprise, he walks to the sink, rinses them out, and places them upside down on the steel counter to dry. He is so mannerly.

'I should be going so,' he says, turning around to look at me but making no attempt to leave. This is not how I expected my day to turn out, but it all seems so natural. I nod, then turn my back on him and walk towards the bedroom. He remains where he is for only a few moments before following me inside and closing the door behind us.

8

BRENDAN WORKED. THE GIRLS grew. I kept busy with the trappings of being an affluent, middle-class woman in South Dublin. I arranged spa days with my friends, had regular appointments with my hairdresser, became – for a time – obsessed with Bikram yoga. I spent at least an hour every morning working on my appearance, choosing what to wear, coordinating and curating my jewellery and fragrances. I maintained an Instagram account, wanting to advertise my perfect life to the world. I forced Brendan to come to the Gate or the Abbey with me whenever there was a new show on. I made reservations for dinner in well-reviewed restaurants. I was very involved with the girls' school, participating in fundraising drives for whatever social problem grabbed our attention. I kept a small champagne fridge in our outside seomra, always well stocked. I thought about building a lifestyle blog and made enquiries of website designers. I was a regular visitor at the National Gallery. I did all the things I felt I was supposed to do to live the perfect life, one that could not have been more different from the one I live now.

We might have lived in Terenure, but the National

Swimming Federation, which was based only a few miles from our front door, was my husband's real home. He spent six days out of seven there and, more often than not, found himself invited to some evening event that meant he wouldn't be home until late. When he finally returned, he'd ignore the meal I'd left for him in the fridge, and wander around the house into the small hours, moving between the living room, his office and the girls' bedrooms, even though they'd be asleep by then. Sometimes I felt as if he was avoiding me entirely, for an hour or more could pass before he came to bed.

Soon after she turned fourteen, I found Emma hovering nearby one morning and turned to look at her. She seemed nervous and jittery, unable to meet my eye. I'd been expecting this for a year or so, and, in preparation for it, had read some articles online on how best to speak to your daughter when the moment came, something my own mother had never done for me, instead simply leaving a box of sanitary towls on my bed and instructing me to read the instructions, throw them away afterwards, and never talk about them to anyone.

'Are you all right?' I asked, and she nodded, then shook her head. I decided there was no point prevaricating. 'Have you started, is that it?'

Now she looked appalled, even insulted.

'No,' she said, rolling her eyes. 'God, I started that last Christmas.'

I was surprised to hear this, even a little wounded that she hadn't confided in me at the time.

'Oh,' I said. 'And it's going all right, is it?'

'It is what it is.'

'You haven't asked me to buy you any tampons.'

'They give them out free at school.'

I nearly fell off the seat at this, but then I had gone to the nuns, and they would have no more discussed the natural functions of the body than they would have done cartwheels across the assembly hall. I'd heard they gave out free condoms to the older students too these days but had avoided telling Brendan this, knowing how he'd react.

'Can you do something for me?' she asked after a pause.

'Of course. What is it?'

'Can you put a lock on my door?'

'Why?' I asked, for it wasn't as if I didn't knock before entering her room and she and Rebecca never argued over taking each other's things, which often seemed like community property between them.

'Because I want one,' she said.

'No, I don't like locks,' I told her, shaking my head. 'What if there was a fire?'

'Then I'd unlock it. Or jump out the window.'

I thought this through. Of course, she was getting older. Perhaps she just needed the illusion of privacy, and I would be wrong to deny her that. Another idea went through my mind, a horrible idea, one that shamed me even to imagine it, and, may God forgive me, I pushed it away. I pushed it far, far away. Why did I not listen to what she was trying to tell me?

'I keep getting woken in the middle of the night,' she said finally.

'By what?' I asked.

'By Dad. When he comes home late.'

'He likes to say goodnight, that's all.'

'But he wakes me up.'

'Well, what if I ask him not to?'

'I'd prefer a lock,' she said, but I still said no. In a year or two, perhaps, I told her. When she was older.

And then, not long after, Brendan returned home to announce that he'd decided to take a sabbatical from his job. He'd left in the morning at the usual time, driven the girls to school, and a few hours later, when I was preparing my lunch, there he was, standing in the kitchen demanding a sandwich. I'd never known him to take so much as a sick day in his life.

'A sabbatical?' I asked. 'I thought that was only something university professors took?'

'Anyone can,' he said. 'I need a break from that place.' He took a bottle of beer from the fridge, which was also out of character as he was never much of a drinker, let alone at lunchtime. 'All the chatter and the politics, it'd drive you to distraction. I've told them I'm taking a few weeks off for myself, to clear my head.'

'But the Olympics,' I began, for the Games were only eighteen months off now and preparations for team selection were in full swing.

'The Olympics will still be there when I get back.'

I stared at him in bewilderment. He'd never so much as suggested to me that he found work stressful. If anything, I'd always thought it was homelife that he didn't enjoy.

'I work too hard,' he said, seeing how puzzled I was. 'Sure don't you always say that yourself?'

'Yes, but—'

'But what? I'll still be getting paid, if that's what you're worried about.'

'That's not it at all,' I said, annoyed by the suggestion. 'I'm just surprised, that's all.'

'Am I messing up your day by being here, is that it?' he asked, growing angry now. 'Would you prefer I went and sat in the library for a few hours or took myself off into town to see a film?'

'Of course not,' I replied, trying to lessen the tension. 'No, I'm just—'

'I've said I'll give them a shout when I'm ready to go back.'

'And they won't give your job away in the meantime?'

'How could they? Sure amn't I too well known for that?'

'Are you depressed?' I asked, sitting down next to him. 'Is that it? Is there anything you'd like to talk about?'

'What I'd like, Vanessa, is *not* to talk about it,' he replied.

'And what will we tell the girls?'

'That I've taken some holiday time that was owing to me. Sure they're too self-involved to care anyway.'

He was right about that at least. By now, Emma and Rebecca were far too involved with the drama of their respective social circles to pay the slightest attention to anything that went on at home. When they realized that their father wasn't going to work, they barely asked any questions, but despite his repeated insistences that I had nothing to worry about, I continued to find the whole thing peculiar.

My confusion was only piqued when I found myself in Dunnes Stores in Cornelscourt a week or so later and ran into Peggy Hartman, whose husband, Seán, was Director of the National Athletics Foundation, a sister organization to Brendan's. I didn't know Peggy well, but our paths had crossed a few times over the years at fundraising benefits and our husbands reported to the same minister, often joining forces when it came to funding applications.

'Peggy,' I said, stopping my trolley halfway along the frozen-food aisle when I saw her coming towards me. 'How are you? I haven't seen you in the longest time.'

I was startled by the expression that crossed her face, which blended embarrassment with anxiety. It was as if I was the very last person she wanted to encounter.

'Vanessa,' she said. 'There you are.'

Peggy and Seán had a son with Down syndrome, and when I asked after him, she told me that he was spending a week with his grandparents in Leitrim, a place he adored.

'That'll give you a break,' I said, perhaps not choosing my words as judiciously as I might have.

'I don't need a break,' she said, surprisingly quick to take offence. 'Why would I?'

'No, of course not,' I replied. 'I only meant that it's hard work, that's all. You must be glad that your parents are happy to take him for a while.'

'He's not a charity case, Vanessa,' she said, and I was startled by her reaction, which was, I thought, unnecessarily defensive.

'No, of course not,' I said. 'I'm sorry, I didn't mean any harm. You're well yourself anyway?'

'I'm fine.'

'And Seán?'

'He's fine too.'

She looked at me coldly and I got the distinct impression that whatever was going on here had nothing to do with what I had just said about her son.

'Is everything all right, Peggy?' I asked. 'If you don't mind me saying, you seem a bit out of sorts.'

She looked around, then shook her head as if she couldn't believe that I'd even have the gall to ask.

'I just don't know what to think,' she said finally.

'About what?'

'Well, there's no smoke without fire, is there?'

I stared at her in bewilderment. She might have been speaking a foreign language for all the sense she was making to me.

'What smoke?' I asked. 'What fire?'

'I think it's best we don't discuss it,' she said. 'Seán has made it clear that I should say nothing.'

'Say nothing about what?'

She shook her head and made to move on, but, before she wheeled her trolley away, she turned back with a look of sympathy on her face.

'Look, I know none of this is your fault,' she said. 'And, of course, it could be nothing more than malicious gossip. I'm just worried that, if it's not, then whatever they discover will be brushed under the carpet.'

'Peggy, I don't—'

'I know from personal experience how that can happen,' she continued, growing more animated now. 'In our day, it didn't matter who you told, they'd just tell you to stop throwing dirt on a good man's reputation and send you away with a flea in your ear, but I thought things had changed in this country. I really did. But it's those men, Vanessa, isn't it? It's those fucking men. They still run everything and look out for each other, no matter what. I hate them. Don't you? And it's women like us who allow it to happen. Because staying quiet is easier than causing a fuss, isn't it? Sometimes I think we're just as bad as they are. Worse.'

She shook her head then, and there were tears in her eyes as she moved on. I didn't follow her. As with the conversation I'd had with Emma about the lock on her door, I blocked it out. Was I being naïve, selfish, or complicit? Was I frightened of investigating this and finding an answer that would destroy us all? I don't know, is the truth, but this is what I've come to the island to ask myself. We'd had an extraordinary conversation and, rather than following Peggy down the aisle and demanding an explanation, I went in search of the Green Isle frozen chips I liked. That seemed more important to me.

Later, I recounted the conversation to Brendan, who listened carefully and remained silent as he considered it, before finally asking at what time of day this had occurred.

'Around half past two,' I told him.

'She's getting earlier, then.'

'Getting earlier at what?'

'Sure, she drinks, that one,' he said. 'Did you not know that?'

'Peggy Hartman?'

'Oh yes. The poor woman has an alcohol problem. Seán told me all about it. I didn't say anything to you because I know you don't like gossip. Apparently she opens her first bottle of wine around four o'clock and that's it, she's on it for the night. But it must be getting worse if she was incoherent after lunch.'

'I never said she was incoherent,' I said. 'She was perfectly articulate. And she certainly wasn't drunk, if that's what you're implying.'

'She knows how to hide it, then,' he replied. 'The alcos are great at hiding it. Trust me, she won't have had the first clue what she was even talking about. She'll have had five stories in her head and been mixing them all up. She'll be lying on her sofa now, sleeping it off. This time tomorrow, she won't even remember having run into you.'

I accepted this and asked no further questions. And when, later that evening, he suggested that the four of us take a trip down to Wexford for a week's holiday since the girls were on half-term anyway, I said yes, great idea, and off we went, swimming in the sea every day because it was a fine spring week. I put Peggy Hartman, her smoke, her fire, and her supposed drink problem, out of my head.

It was while we were in White's that the phone call came. Brendan and I were having a drink in the hotel bar when one of the waiters said he had a call at reception. I wondered who might be calling him there, who even knew what hotel we had come to, and before he stood up, Brendan did something uncharacteristic. Looking like a man about to face his executioner, he placed a hand on top of my own and held it there for a moment, as if we were courting for the first time all over again, and offered a sad smile before leaving the bar and making his way into the lobby.

I sat still, telling myself not to worry, that whatever it was would be something trivial. The call seemed to take an eternity, but it couldn't have been more than a few minutes until he returned, looking excited and relieved.

'What was that all about?' I asked as he sat down, ordering us another round.

'The credit-card company, that's all,' he told me. 'They wanted to check it was really me spending money here.'

'Right,' I said, wondering how they would have tracked him down if that was the case. Wouldn't they have rung his mobile? We remained silent for a few minutes before Brendan spoke again.

'Is it just me?' he asked. 'Or are holidays overrated?'

'I wouldn't know,' I said. 'We rarely take any.'

'Sure haven't we had five days here already?' he asked. 'Maybe we'll skip the last two, will we? Head back up to Dublin tomorrow morning? I might drop into work in the afternoon.'

'You're going back?'

'It's time, I think. We'll tell the girls later, will we? Get them to pack their things tonight? If we set off after breakfast, we could be home by one.'

'All right,' I said.

Could I not have asked him then? Could I not have insisted on knowing the truth about that phone call and why he'd taken this sabbatical so unexpectedly, and then ended it without warning? Could I not have said, *Brendan, I know there's something you're not telling me, and you'll say it now or I will ring the National Swimming Federation myself and find out*? Could I not have done that?

I could have, of course, but I didn't.

Why didn't I? What was wrong with me? Willow would have demanded answers; Vanessa couldn't even form the questions.

In the end, he didn't go back to work the next day, or, indeed, for the next two weeks, because we woke the following morning to the sound of Rebecca knocking on our door to tell us that Emma wasn't in her bed, that she'd been searching the hotel for her and could find her nowhere. Neither Brendan nor I were particularly concerned – she was always taking herself off somewhere and we assumed she'd just gone for a walk in Wexford town – but by the time I was dressed and downstairs, Rebecca was conspicuously anxious and, to alleviate her concerns, I said that we'd go look for her.

And that was when two Gardaí came through the door and made their way to reception to ask whether there was a Mr and Mrs Carvin in residence. The woman behind the desk pointed us out and the younger of the

Gardaí, who didn't look like he was long out of short trousers, turned around with an expression on his face that suggested the conversation ahead was not going to be a happy one. When he caught my eye, he knew in that moment that I was the mother, and I knew exactly what he was going to tell me.

And even after that, I still asked no questions.

It's women like us who allow it to happen. That's what Peggy Hartman had said. *Because staying quiet is easier than causing a fuss, isn't it?*

9

I'M IN THE OLD pub, reading a novel, when Tim Devlin walks in. He stops and looks me up and down, as if I'm a car or a piece of livestock that he's considering putting in an offer on, and I stare back, challenging his gaze, but neither of us says a word. Instead, he makes his way towards the bar and orders a pint of Guinness before walking back towards me.

'Do you mind if I join you?' he asks.

I haven't spoken to anyone in almost a week, and realize that I'm in need of human contact, so I put my bookmark in its place and indicate the seat next to me.

'I thought you and I were never going to talk,' I tell him.

'Well, one of us needs to make the first move, I suppose,' he replies, a phrase that bothers me. Does he think we've been dancing around each other all this time, waiting for the right moment? If he does, he would be wrong. 'Let me get you another drink first,' he adds, seeing my almost empty glass. 'What's that, a white wine?'

'Yes,' I say, and he puts his pint down, then returns to the bar, where he chats briefly with the publican. I wonder what sort of relationship they have, these two men supposedly in competition with each other. It's a small island of only four hundred people, but perhaps those four hundred have a rare thirst on them so there's enough business to go around.

'Now then,' he says when he returns, taking the stool opposite me rather than joining me on the banquette. 'I don't think I've introduced myself, have I? Tim Devlin.'

'Willow Hale,' I say. 'So, what made you decide to talk to me today?'

'I've been serving you soups and sandwiches for months now,' he replies, 'and we never exchange more than a hello and a goodbye. It's got a little awkward, don't you think?'

'A little,' I agree, finishing my first glass of wine and starting on the second.

'I had the impression from the start that you wanted to be left alone.'

'I did, for the most part. You probably thought I was the rudest woman in Ireland.'

'Oh no,' he replies, shaking his head. 'I already met her. Sure I was married to her daughter for years.'

I laugh, despite myself. A mother-in-law joke. I thought they'd gone out with the ark.

'This island seems to draw us in, doesn't it?' I say.

'Us?'

'The forlorn.'

'What makes you think I'm forlorn?' he asks.

'You wear your loneliness like an overcoat,' I tell him. 'It's one of the reasons I haven't talked to you either. I always assume you just want to get on with your work without any fuss.'

'That's true enough.'

'Can I guess?'

'Can you guess what?'

'What you're struggling with.'

He shrugs.

'If you want,' he says.

'You were a bad husband,' I say. 'You drank or you gambled. Maybe you cheated. In the end, your wife divorced you and it was only then that you realized what you'd thrown away. You've regretted your actions ever since, but she met someone else in the meantime and wouldn't return to you, so you came here, to the island, to disappear.'

'Not bad,' he tells me, nodding his head. 'Although my wife didn't divorce me. She died.'

I have the good grace to look ashamed of myself.

'I'm sorry,' I say. 'That was flippant of me.'

'You don't need to apologize,' he replies, waving this away.

I wonder whether I'm supposed to ask how his wife died but, before I can, he changes the subject.

'And you,' he says. 'How are you enjoying life on the island?'

'The first few months weren't easy,' I tell him. 'I found the isolation strange. But now, well, I'm worried that I'm becoming institutionalized. Although I feel quite content most days. So maybe that's not such a bad thing.'

'Content enough to stay?'

'Not for ever, no. But for a time. When I arrived, my head was quite . . . how shall I put this? Messy.'

'And now it's clean?'

'Cleaner than it was anyway. There's something about long walks, little social interaction and no Wi-Fi that does wonders for the soul.'

'It's why I have no router in the new pub,' he tells me. 'I don't want people sitting on their phones, Twittering away or checking their Facebooks or any of that shite.'

'I never understood the appeal of all that,' I tell him. 'Sharing every random thought or interaction we have with the world. Don't most people prefer privacy?'

'You're better off not being on it,' he says, leaning forward and lowering his voice. 'When you come under the kind of scrutiny you came under, it must be corrosive to the soul. All those strangers attacking you, calling you names, thinking they know you when they don't have the first clue. Using you to alleviate their personal misery and sense of failure.'

I turn my head to my right, towards the wall, and close my eyes for a moment. When I open them again, I find that I'm looking directly at a framed poster of *Man of Aran*, the Robert Flaherty documentary, that looks as if it's been hanging there since the dawn of time. A confident man with a hoop of rope is staring at the camera, penetrating the lens with his masculinity. To his right, a little behind him, visibly subservient, stands his wife, strands of hair blowing into her eyes. She has no expectations of life.

'You know who I am, then,' I say finally, turning back to him, resigned to my unmasking.

'I've known who you were since the first moment you

walked through my door,' he says. 'But I didn't like to say anything. I didn't want to frighten you off, for one thing. And it was none of my business.'

'Have you told anyone?' I ask.

'I haven't, no. I would never do something like that.'

A silence descends upon us. Part of me wants to leave; another part wants to unburden myself of my secrets, for who else do I have to confide in, after all? Rebecca refuses to answer any of my messages. *I'm not cutting you off for ever*, her actions tell me. *But I will only talk to you when I'm ready, and then it will be on my own terms.*

'The first thing I did when I arrived on the island was change my name and cut my hair,' I tell Tim, deciding to let some of my horrible story escape into the world. 'I scalped it right down, as you can see. It doesn't seem to be growing back either, which both worries me and doesn't bother me in the slightest, if that makes any sense.'

'Why your hair?' he asks.

'I didn't want anyone to recognize me. I've been in the papers so much over the last year and I wanted to be anonymous. Believe me, when you achieve a certain amount of fame or notoriety in this country, there are days when you long to have a different face or be a different person entirely. Just to keep the jackals away. A stranger arriving on the island would inevitably attract interest and I didn't want to give myself away too easily so I had to make some changes.'

'Most people don't read the papers here,' he tells me. 'You've probably noticed that Con Dwyer only gets in a dozen or so copies of the *Irish Times* and the *Indo* every day. And even those are always a day late. No, we have enough problems of our own to worry about here without bothering about what goes on over there.' He nods in the vague direction of the mainland.

'Perhaps I'm overestimating my celebrity,' I say.

'Well, they're not ignorant,' he adds. 'They'd know the story, the islanders, if you asked them. Sure it was all over the news. They just might not recognize the players.'

'"They", not "we"?' I ask.

He shrugs, perhaps uncertain if he's ready to fully align himself with this community. Is he an outsider too, then?

'I wasn't sure it would be enough,' I tell him. 'The haircut, I mean. But I seem to have got away with it. At least I thought I had. Until now.'

'I've always been a great man for the sport,' he tells me. 'So, a story like yours—'

'Not mine, my husband's.'

'When it rears its ugly head, I pay attention. Twelve years, wasn't it? That's what he got?'

I drink half my glass of wine in one gulp. I don't get the sense that he's being unkind, or that he's prying. He's simply talking to me.

'That's right,' I say.

'So, what, he'll be in his mid-seventies when he gets out?'

'He won't serve the full term if he behaves well.'

'Does he have a history of behaving well?'

The look I give him probably says it all.

'Are you worried that the other prisoners will hurt

him? They don't take kindly to people who do what he did.'

He's right about this, and it bothers me that, yes, I am. It does concern me. I've known Brendan more than half my life, after all, and I know how vulnerable he must be in prison. He's not a strong man. He liked power, and authority, and fame, but he's weak at heart. I don't love him, I don't even like him, but he's part of me. We created a family together and destroyed it together. Despite the terrible things he's done, it's very difficult to abandon those feelings entirely. I know he will be constantly frightened. But then, those eight little girls – the eight that we know of, anyway; I have no doubt that there were many more – he has caused unspeakable damage in their lives. If he were killed in prison, that would be celebrated by most. How can I explain, to myself, to anyone, the fact that I would weep?

'I'm sure the wardens will keep charge,' I say weakly.

'You don't understand the prison eco-system,' he tells me. 'There's not much difference between the wardens and the prisoners. It's just hundreds of men all stuck together inside a big stone building, some getting paid for the privilege, some not. Some sleeping in cells, some going home of an evening.'

I catch the barman's eye and raise my eyebrows to indicate that I'd like to order another round. When it arrives, Tim downs the final quarter of his Guinness, before standing up and carrying our empty glasses to the bar. I like the fact that he'd never make another barman clear up after him.

'You've been to prison, haven't you?' I ask when he returns. I'm determined to keep my voice steady, even if his crime was something heinous. I don't want him to think that I'm frightened of him. I refuse to be frightened of men any more.

'I spent six years in Mountjoy,' he admits. 'I came here the day after my release.'

'Do you mind if I ask what you did?'

'No. Most people on the island know anyway. I'm surprised no one's told you, to be honest.'

'I find that people here are very discreet.'

'True enough. Drink driving.' He looks down at the table that separates us and scratches the woodwork with the nail of his thumb. 'My wife and I had been out for the night and I was supposed to leave the car behind and collect it the next day, but we'd had a row about something stupid and when she tried to take the keys off me, I got lairy with her and insisted on driving us home. She should have refused to come with me and took a taxi home instead, but no. I don't remember anything after that. All I know is I woke up in St James's Hospital the next day to be told that I'd escaped the crash with barely a scratch but that my wife was dead. Which explained why my left wrist was handcuffed to the bedframe and a young Garda was sitting next to the bed reading *The Da Vinci Code*.'

I wonder should I offer condolences but decide not to. He is the author of his own misfortune, after all. Is it any wonder he looked so distressed in the church that day?

'And you loved her,' I say, uncertain whether I mean this as a question or a statement.

'I did,' he replies.

'Did you have children?'

'A young lad, yeah. Well, not so young any more. He lives with his aunt. My wife's sister. He won't see me. I don't blame him. You lost a daughter too, am I right?'

This unsettles me. An estranged son and a dead daughter are not the same thing. Also, it's starting to grate on me that he knows so much about my life.

'My daughter took her own life,' I tell him. 'I have another, Rebecca. But right now, she's not talking to me either.'

'I'm sorry,' he says.

'I hoped this time apart would be good for us,' I continue. 'That she would miss me. Worry about me, even. But I don't think she does. I think she'd prefer that I never return.'

'Does she talk to your husband?'

'Ex-husband. And no, she doesn't. And whether or not she ever reconciles with me, I know she'll never speak to him again. I know that with absolute certainty.'

'She blames him, then.'

'For abusing all those children? Of course she does. Why wouldn't she?'

'No, I mean she blames him for her sister's suicide.'

I'm surprised to find myself having such a personal conversation with a relative stranger. I've never had such a conversation before. And yet, I keep going. At this point, I have nothing to lose. And it feels good to speak about something that I've been hiding since boarding the ferry in Galway all those months ago.

'Yes,' I say.

'She thinks he did it to her too.'

'Yes.'

'And do you?'

'Yes.'

'So she blames you for that?'

'Yes.'

He breathes heavily through his nose, as if all the pain of the world is bottled up inside him, desperate for release, then stands up and goes to the bar, where he orders more drinks without bothering to ask whether I want one. I still have almost a full glass of wine before me, but I drink it down, enjoying how it numbs me from the inside. I don't want him to outpace me.

'It's a terrible thing, guilt,' he says, when he sets the drinks down before us. 'I have nightmares sometimes. Do you?'

'No,' I lie.

'I thought everyone who suffered a trauma did.'

'Not me.'

We remain silent for a few moments.

'What was it like?' I ask eventually.

'What was what like?'

'When you woke up in the hospital and they told you what you'd done. How did you feel?'

He looks out into the centre of the bar and considers it. A few more people have come in by now. Some I recognize from my wanderings around the village. Some are strangers to me. Two, I think, are tourists, for the summer season has just begun. They are, without question,

American, and seem to think they've walked on to a film set. The woman immediately takes her camera out and starts snapping photographs. When she turns and aims it in our direction, I tell her, in no uncertain terms, not to press that button.

'How did I feel?' says Tim, when the Americans have scattered to the other end of the pub in fright. 'I felt as if my entire life had been leading towards that moment. The truth is, I was always what might be called a dissolute youth. I drank. I took drugs. I womanized. I was not always kind to people. I was certainly not kind to my parents, God rest them. I stole from my employer and got away with it. Just small amounts, but they added up over time. I cheated on my wife for no other reason than I could and because I believed I was entitled to as much sex as I could get, with as many people as would have me. When I was in my late twenties, I was rougher with a girl in this regard than I should have been. She lodged no complaint with the Gardaí, but I remember what I did, and I think about it often. And the party we were at, the night of the accident, was a birthday party for the wife of a good friend, and I'd been seeing that woman secretly for months. My problem is, I don't think I ever understood how to be an adult. In my heart, I still feel like a teenage boy. So you ask how did I feel? I feel that there was an inevitability to it all. The moment I was told what I had done, I made my peace with the fact that I would be going to prison and, even then, lying in that hospital bed, I began to think about the changes I would make when I was eventually released. I resolved to be a better man.'

He returns to his pint now and glances up at me cautiously as if he expects me to reach across and place my hand atop his, to commend him for his honesty and tell him that he must forgive himself, that his wife would not want him to live with such guilt, and that he must learn to live again. I can see this in his face and wonder whether he has told this same story to other women, and they have comforted him in this way. But I refuse, I absolutely refuse, to comply. He can anticipate his cathartic moment all he likes, but I won't be providing it.

'*I don't think I ever understood how to be an adult,*' I say, mimicking him. '*In my heart, I still feel like a teenage boy.* But that's the problem with men like you, isn't it? You refuse to accept that you're not, in fact, a teenage boy, any more than you're a cow or a sheep. You're nearly sixty, for God's sake. You think the world has treated you cruelly by forcing you to age. But the women, we're not allowed to act like teenage girls, are we? No, we become wives and mothers and we try to keep our families together and we make excuses for these infantilized beings we call husbands. Have you listened to yourself? Your first thought when you woke up in that hospital was to fast-forward to years after your trial, years after your imprisonment, all the way to your release, and who you would be then and what you would do. Not a thought in your head for the poor woman you'd killed and to whom you'd, presumably, once offered words of love and a lifetime of fidelity. Just the endless selfishness of the middle-aged man who does whatever he wants and leaves his wife to pick up the pieces. I don't doubt your grief,

Tim, or your guilt. But God Almighty, will men like you ever stop telling stories like this and asking the world to excuse you, because you still feel like a teenage boy and, somehow, you can't help yourself? You *could* help yourself if you just grew the fuck up and behaved like an adult, which is what you are. But you choose not to. Do you hear what I'm telling you? Tim? Are you listening to me? Do you hear what I'm saying?'

10

THERE'S A FLURRY OF activity on the beach, and I make my way along the path towards the spot where a group of islanders has gathered. In amongst them is Luke's mother, concealed beneath so many layers that it might be the dead of winter and not a clear summer's evening. I wonder if she knows that her son and I had sex, and that we continue to, whenever the mood takes us. I don't for a moment imagine that he would have confided in her, but mothers, some mothers anyway, have a way of intuiting these things.

'Mrs Duggan,' I say, and she looks me up and down as if there is so much wrong with me that she wouldn't even know where to begin. 'What's going on?'

'Evan Keogh,' she replies. 'He took off early for Galway and hasn't been seen since.'

The name rings a bell, but I can't quite place it until, at last, I remember her mentioning him to me when she first came to remonstrate with me for feeding Bananas. A talented footballer, if I remember correctly. Didn't his father want him to go to England for a trial with one of the clubs there?

'Took off in what way?' I ask. 'Not swimming, I

presume?' If the boy's been out swimming since morning, I'm not surprised there's concern. I've read of charity swims between the island and Doolin, so I suppose a distance like that is possible. But Doolin is only ten miles from here, while Galway is twenty-four. Only a fool would attempt such a thing without a vessel following in case of an emergency.

'Ah, no,' she says. 'He took Charlie's boat out, and he's never done that before. Not on his own anyway. And neither sight nor sound of him since.'

I look out across the waves, as if I will see the missing boy surfing towards me on the horizon.

'He couldn't have got into difficulty, surely,' I say. 'It's been such a fine day. No wind at all.'

'Accidents happen,' she replies with all the pessimism that women like her revel in. 'Better things have happened to worse men.'

A little further along, within a circle of protective friends, stands a middle-aged woman looking pale and frightened, even annoyed. I take her to be Mrs Keogh, who I recognize from the knit shop in the village. I bought a scarf from her a few weeks after I arrived and it's a thing of beauty, made from Merino wool, with intersecting threads of turquoise and tangerine. I wear it on cold evenings if I'm going to the old pub for a meal. One of the women tries to place a consolatory arm around her shoulder but she shrugs it off and marches down towards the shore, fierce in her stride, to where the tide rolls in. She's beseeching the water to go against its nature, to show compassion for once, but, like King

Canute demanding that the tides fall still, she's asking in vain, for water is the cruellest of all the elements and will swallow up anyone who challenges it.

'Has someone gone looking for him?' I ask.

'Charlie's gone, of course. And my Luke, along with two of his pals. They're away an hour since. We'll stay here now till they all get back safe, God willing.'

A part of me wants to return to the cottage and hide under the bedsheets. I cannot be here if the men return with bad news, as those two Gardaí did for me on that long-ago holiday in Wexford. I cannot witness any mirroring of my grief.

I remember a small van that, since the arrival of the summer tourists, is usually parked at the top of the dunes, selling teas and coffees, ice creams and soft drinks from a window hatch, and I make my way back up to the road and walk in its direction, hoping it will still be there, despite the hour. Sure enough, it is, although when I reach it, the girl inside is packing up for the night.

'Are you still serving?' I ask, and she glances towards the hot-water urn, pressing a hand briefly against its steel surface, before nodding.

'You just caught me,' she says. 'And it's still hot. What will you have?'

'A large tea,' I tell her. 'Strong and sweet.'

She takes the largest of the Styrofoam cups from a shelf behind her and drops in a tea bag before filling it with steaming water and reaching for the bag of sugar.

'How many?' she asks.

'Two,' I say, handing across a couple of euros and

taking the cup from her, pressing the lid in place, and walking back towards the beach. To my surprise, Mrs Keogh has separated herself from the ghoulish gathering and is now alone in the dunes, her arms folded before her. I approach cautiously and clear my throat so as not to surprise her. When she turns to look at me, she blinks a little, as if she's just woken from a dream.

'I brought you some tea,' I say, handing it across. 'I put some sugar in it. I'd have put whiskey in if I'd any to hand.'

'That's kind of you,' she says, taking it and warming her hands on the cup's surround.

'Would you like me to leave you alone?' I ask, conscious that she might have changed position for privacy's sake, but she shakes her head.

'Stay if you like,' she says. 'This is all a lot of fuss over nothing. Evan's a good sailor. No harm could come to him on a day like this. He'll have docked on a beach somewhere and gone into the town for the afternoon.'

'I don't doubt it,' I say, wanting to reassure her.

'He'll come sailing back any minute now and throw a fit over why we're all acting like he's drowned.'

I bristle a little at the casual use of the word but decide not to pick her up on it. I don't know if she's trying to persuade herself or me.

'We haven't met, have we?' she says eventually, sipping on the tea.

'Not really,' I say. 'Although I've been in your shop. I'm Willow Hale.'

'Maggie Keogh. You're famous, you know.'

I frown, unsettled by this remark.

'Sure everybody was talking about you when you first arrived,' she explains. 'The Pope himself wouldn't have garnered so much interest. A woman from Dublin and not a husband in sight!' She indicates the men and women gathered on the shore before us, who seem to have forgotten about her and are locked in chat as they wait to see how this drama will play out. 'That's what they were all saying anyway. Gossips, the lot of them. They drive me around the bend with their nonsense.'

Something in her voice makes me realize that she is not a native islander.

'Where are you from?' I ask.

'Wicklow,' she tells me. 'I met Charlie when I was too young to know any better and allowed him to drag me here.'

There's so much bitterness in her tone that it shocks me. It makes me think that she is already anticipating the worst and has adopted the persona of the grieving mother earlier than necessary. Each of us does it differently, of course.

She takes her phone from her pocket and taps a couple of numbers on the screen before lifting it to her ear, waiting a moment, then sighing in frustration as she returns it to her pocket.

'This is what I don't understand,' she says, looking to me as if I can offer an explanation. 'He never turns his phone off. Evan, I mean. He has it on him all day long and he always answers. And now it's just going to voicemail. What does that mean, do you think? Might it have been stolen from him?'

Until now, I have assumed that the islanders are merely creating a commotion to give their day a bit of excitement, but this makes me wonder. Perhaps the boy has come to mischief, after all. I take my own phone from my pocket, open the messaging service, and there is Rebecca's photograph, only it's changed again. Now it is a picture taken from behind, and she is standing much like I am, on a dune somewhere, looking out to sea. Which sea is this, I wonder? And what is she doing there? I check when she was last online. An hour ago. I type a message.

I miss you. I am well.

I wait to see that she has received and read it before returning the phone to my pocket, hoping for the sound of a reply but anticipating none. Maggie Keogh looks at me.

'Who were you texting?' she asks.

'My daughter,' I say.

'Do you have just the one?'

I find this a complicated question to answer. The intimacy of the truth would be too much in the present moment.

'Yes,' I tell her. 'Rebecca.'

'She didn't come here with you?'

'Oh no,' I say. 'She'd go out of her mind in a place like this.'

'Sure we all do that,' says Maggie. 'Most of us lost our minds long ago. Would it surprise you to know that I haven't set foot on the mainland in eight years?'

'Why not?' I ask her.

'He won't let me,' she says.

'Who won't?'

'Charlie.'

'I don't understand.'

She shrugs her shoulders, as if she's long since stopped thinking about it. 'Neither do I,' she says.

What a strange existence, I think, to spend so much of one's life in a place like this, ruled by the whims of a man, and to know so little of the world. Never to have climbed the Eiffel Tower, or walked across the Sydney Harbour Bridge, or stared into the depths of the Grand Canyon. To settle for a barren rock in the Atlantic Ocean where you could probably spend a lifetime and encounter only a few hundred different faces. I think of those Japanese soldiers who lasted for decades on small islands in the Pacific, still believing the war was going on.

'So he's run away,' I say. 'Your son, I mean. He's escaping his father.'

'He's frightened.'

'Of your husband?'

She looks at me with an expression on her face that's difficult to read. This is a woman who needs to unburden herself of something. 'Partly,' she says.

'You don't have to tell me,' I say, stating the obvious. 'It's your business. Did I hear that he wants to be a professional footballer?'

Maggie laughs bitterly. 'He has the talent, that's for sure,' she tells me. 'You've never seen such skill with a ball. But he doesn't want it. He has no interest in the game. His father is all for it, though. He likes the idea of

Evan lining up in Lansdowne Road, singing "Amhrán na bhFiann" at the top of his voice as the television cameras pass by.'

'And what does Evan want?'

'To paint, apparently.'

'Is he good?'

'I don't know,' she says, her face filled with emotion.

'But you've seen his paintings, I presume?'

'Oh. You meant his art.'

'What else would I mean?'

She smiles now and shakes her head. 'That's the problem,' she says. 'I don't think he is. He doesn't have the talent to do what he wants but he has the talent to do what he doesn't want. So there's a conundrum for you.'

I nod. 'Yes,' I say.

'They all think he's drowned,' she continues, nodding towards our neighbours. 'But he hasn't. He's run away, that's all. He's frightened. He's hiding. I hope they don't catch him. Let him go to Dublin or London or somewhere further afield and escape all this.' She waves her hand around, as if conjuring a spell. 'I should have done it myself long ago.'

She closes her eyes, breathing in the cool evening air as if desperate to cleanse her lungs. I consider placing my hand on her arm to comfort her when a roar rises from the beach and we both startle, looking out towards the horizon, where the sun is starting to set.

'It's them,' she says, and, sure enough, a small boat can be seen in the distance making its way towards the shore. She drops the cup in the marram grass that protrudes from the sand and the lid falls off, tea spilling out and darkening the sand like a spreading sin, before making her way hurriedly in the direction of the water. I reach down to pick the cup up, unable to litter a beach, and follow her. Like the neighbours that I'm so quick to condemn, I'm eager to know how this evening's story ends.

There's a sharp buzz among them as the boat draws closer, and I can see the large handsome shape of my lover, Luke, on board. We have formed an easy friendship, based on conversation, intimacy, sex and a mutual understanding that neither of us wants anything more from the other than what we are willing to give. It is uncomplicated and it is welcome.

Behind Luke, I can make out his two friends, and an older man, sitting near the stern, with a cap pulled down over his forehead. I take him to be Charlie Keogh, and he does not look like a brute, but, of course, appearances can be deceptive. I blink, thinking I must have missed someone, and look at each again in turn. I want to tell someone, to shout that the boy is missing, drowned, dead, but who am I to spread such a terrible alarm? If the worst has happened, then let Maggie Keogh enjoy what time is left to her before she is forced to become a – what? There are widows. And widowers. And orphans. But there is no word to define a parent who loses a child. The language is missing a noun. Perhaps because it is so unnatural.

The babble dies down when the boat pulls into the shore, and no one moves as they see what I have seen and make their own calculations. I catch Luke's eye and offer him an expression of support. I admire this heroic side to his character, the young man who will take to the water to search for a missing islander. His friends rise and then, behind them, hidden from view until now, I see the boy. The crowd howls in relief as he pulls himself to his feet, looking around in fury and humiliation. Even from here, I can see the black eye that is blossoming on his face, no doubt the result of his father's violence. He waits until only Luke is left on board before stepping on to land, and I wonder where his boat is, the one on which he tried to make his escape. In Galway? Or sunk? How has he left in one vessel and returned in another?

And I see his face even more clearly as he turns and looks in my direction, unwilling to accept the embraces of those who have known him since birth. Our eyes meet and I realize that he is the boy I saw in the church that day. The boy who went to confession in the certainty that he had sinned.

His mother runs towards him, her arms outstretched, but he will not allow her to enfold him. Instead, he charges up the dunes, his runners finding quick purchase in the sand, and disappears over the top, to a place where he can be neither seen nor hurt.

II

A GENERAL ELECTION IS taking place and a politician visits to address the voters he hasn't laid eyes on in almost five years. His appearance offers a timely interruption to the repetitious nature of our lives, so most of us gather in the church to hear him speak, where the sense of excitement is completely out of proportion to the identity of our visitor.

I showed up under the impression that we were to be addressed by a young woman standing for one of the five Galway West seats for the first time, but, when the doors are closed and the welcoming party ascends the altar steps, I'm horrified to see that she has been replaced by a more senior member of her party, a fellow named Jack Sharkey, the current Minister for Tourism, Culture, Arts, the Gaeltacht, Sport and Media. I've known Jack for many years, since long before his elevation to the Cabinet. In fact, it was while he was a humble TD in a previous administration that he, along with Gareth Wilson, pushed for Brendan to be created Director of the National Swimming Federation. Many human dominoes toppled after my husband's disgrace, but somehow Jack has remained standing.

Ifechi may have loaned his church to accommodate the speech, but naturally he cannot be seen to have any involvement in party politics, so he is perhaps the only islander to be absent, and his place is taken by Larry Mulshay, proprietor of the old pub and the unofficial mayor of the island. Leaning too close to the microphone, Larry welcomes us before announcing that the young woman we had been expecting was unable to make it, but we should be honoured that Mr Sharkey has come instead. I can tell this is a lie. Jack probably heard about this evening and, knowing the constituency to be finely balanced, decided that the votes of four hundred people could make the difference between election and unemployment, so used his influence to keep his colleague on the mainland. Either that, or he tipped her into the water on the ferry over. We are also informed that, while we're all entitled to our own political viewpoints, Larry is certain that we will listen to Mr Sharkey – Jack – politely and be respectful in our questions afterwards.

It is as if we are children gathered in an assembly hall, being instructed by the headteacher that any transgression will land us in trouble. I half expect him to remove a cane from his sleeve and patrol the pews, watchful for any gum-chewing or illicit texting.

I am in the sixth row, two places removed from the aisle, and I sink down in my seat, hoping that Jack will not catch my eye. I'm not certain that he would recognize me, but it's not impossible. Over the years, we've been in each other's company on perhaps half a dozen occasions, and he was the subject of multiple enquiries from the media during Brendan's trial, so no doubt observed it closely, lest he be dragged before an Oireachtas committee to explain his early support for my husband. Still, my current appearance is far removed from the glamorous wife he might remember, if he remembers me at all, so my new-found invisibility to the male gaze is an asset.

He takes to the microphone now in a more professional manner and thanks us all for coming. He tells a few politician-mocking jokes that sound as if they've been trotted out multiple times over the years. He's from Galway himself, of course, Oughterard, and speaks of his abiding love for these islands and for this island in particular. His voice cracks when he recounts stories of summer holidays he spent here as a boy with his sainted parents, now gone to their eternal reward, then looks down at the floor as if he's not sure that he can go on, but then, somehow, like Beckett, he goes on.

He talks of agriculture. He talks of emigration. He talks of civil war politics. He talks of NATO. He talks of the Gardaí. He talks of hospital beds. He talks of the elite up there in Dublin. He talks of farmers. He talks of bricklayers. He talks of class sizes. He talks of carbon emissions. He talks of the British prime minister. He talks of Brexit. He talks of the pandemic. He talks of his father, who represented this constituency before him. He talks of a close friend who is black. He talks of a niece who is embracing a male identity. He talks of young people and of why they are our greatest natural resource. He talks of solar power. He talks of the GAA. He talks of Bono and Sinéad O'Connor. He talks of fishing quotas.

He talks, in English, of his love for the Irish language. He talks, in Irish, of his love for Manchester United. He talks of his admiration for women. He talks of the EU. He talks of Emmanuel Macron. He talks of his Cabinet colleagues. He talks of RTÉ bias. He talks of *Ulysses*, and *The Commitments*, and *Normal People*, and of how Irish writers have given so much to the world. He talks of Michael D. He talks of the Eurovision Song Contest. He talks of the rise of populism across Europe. He talks of Ukraine. He talks of his hernia operation.

And just when I think he will talk for ever, that we will all grow old and die here, that our bodies will decompose and slowly turn to dust while he continues to talk and talk and talk, he stops, and his audience delivers a loud round of applause, as if to say that, whatever he might have planned next, he can forget it, because we consider this the end of his talk.

He appears to accept this and takes his place on a high stool that I recognize from the old pub and sips a glass of water while a roving mic is brought around the audience. Anxiously, we await the brave soul who might accept it first.

When a question comes, it is from the mother of an autistic son who asks when more resources will be provided for boys like her Tomás. His teacher, she says, is a wonderful man but he simply cannot cope with her son's special needs. It's not his fault; he doesn't have the training. What can be done, she wants to know? And when will it be done? Jack asks the appropriate questions in reply, pretending to care, before saying that this is a question for his good friend, the Minister for Education, and that if she gives her details to his assistant later, he will make sure that someone from that department is in touch soon.

Before the woman can speak again, the microphone is ripped from her hands and given to an elderly man who I have seen sinking pint after pint of Guinness in the new pub and who wants to know how Jack voted in the Equal Rights Marriage Referendum of 2015.

'Sure that was years ago now, wasn't it?' says Jack, laughing a little, and an uncomfortable frisson passes through the room. 'I can barely remember what I had for my dinner last night.' Whatever it was, I think, he went back for seconds.

The man insists on an answer. He says that he grew up in a Catholic country, but politicians have turned it into Sodom and Gomorrah, and that John Charles McQuaid would turn in his grave if he saw what a den of iniquity this once holy land has turned into. Fellas kissing fellas, he says. And girls kissing girls. In public! On the street! Without an ounce of shame! And half of them don't even know if they're a fella or a girl! Was it for this that the men of 1916 fought and died, he blathers on, and I take a moment to examine my nails and notice they need cutting.

Jack hears him out but takes his time to formulate a reply.

'I voted no,' he tells us eventually. 'At the time, I considered marriage to be a sacred institution between a man and woman. And while I am proud to have voted with my conscience, I'm not convinced that I would vote the same way again, although perhaps I would. Or maybe not. Yes, men are now free to marry men, and women are free to marry women, but the world does not seem to have fallen off its axis since the legislation was passed. The fact is, we need to move with the times while recognizing that, sometimes, the old ways are best.'

In his search for an answer that will satisfy no one and everyone in equal parts, I have to concede that Jack has succeeded admirably. He is a politician down to his fingernails.

A third question emerges, this one an obvious plant from a supporter. The man wants to know: if Jack is Minister for Tourism, Culture, Arts, the Gaeltacht, Sport and Media, then what in God's name does he do on the seventh day? The audience laughs appreciatively, pleased to have moved on to a less contentious topic, and Jack tells us that even the good Lord rested on Sunday and that surely no one, not even his political opponents, would begrudge him a day off.

More questions follow, some anodyne, some pugnacious, until finally a young woman who serves behind the counter in Con Dwyer's newsagent's rises to her feet and takes the microphone, holding it nervously but defiantly in her hands, like a contestant on a television singing competition.

'My name is Lucy Wood,' she says, 'and I'll be a first-time voter in this election.'

There's a predictable round of applause for this and Lucy blushes a little, but, I notice, she does not smile. She does, however, wear a determined expression on her face.

'Many people in this country know what it is to face sexual abuse,' she begins.

From behind me, a man mutters, 'Ah, for God's sake.'

'I've faced it myself,' she continues into the disapproving silence. 'So I want to ask you a question in relation to your support of Brendan Carvin. You appointed him as Director of the National Swimming Federation in 2004, isn't that right?'

I feel my heart begin to pound faster in my chest. I have studiously avoided catching Jack's eye since he appeared on the altar steps and have no intention of looking up now.

'No, that decision did not fall to me,' replies Jack after a pause. 'Although I was party to it, as I have admitted on many occasions over the last year. It is to my eternal regret that I was. It is a cross that I have to bear.'

It's interesting to me that he immediately casts himself in the role of the victim. Also, this is the second time he has compared himself to a member of the Holy Trinity. Messianic complexes, I'm sure, are rife in his line of work.

'So, that being the case,' continues Lucy, ignoring his last comment, 'do you have anything to say to those eight little girls who that man abused?'

'Leave it alone, sure what's done is done!' cries a voice from a few rows behind me that I recognize immediately as belonging to Mrs Duggan. She is not alone in her desire for this subject to be dropped; several others chime in too. And inside, silently, so do I.

'Naturally, my heart goes out to those young women—'

'No, they weren't young women,' insists Lucy with a lawyer's need for precision. 'They were children.'

'Yes, indeed. Children,' agrees Jack. 'And I hope they find the healing they need in the years ahead. With God's help—'

'Oh, fuck off,' says another voice, one I do not recognize, from the rear of the church, but it is a youthful, male voice. I have nothing to base this on, but somehow I think it might be the voice of Evan Keogh.

'With God's help, they will get past whatever might have happened to them.'

'*Might* have happened to them?' asks Lucy, growing angry now.

'*Did* happen to them, according to the courts,' says Jack, correcting himself, and I marvel at how he can make an entirely accurate remark sound as if he's casting doubt upon the verdict.

'But at his trial,' continues Lucy, and, finally looking up, I see the growing indignation on Jack's face. He didn't come here to be challenged by an eighteen-year-old girl. He came to trot out his stump speech and drink a few pints of Guinness later with people he thought could ensure his re-election. 'At his trial, you said, and I quote' – and here she unfolds a newspaper clipping she has brought with her – '*Brendan Carvin was a great gift to Irish swimming. Fiercely proud of his young swimmers, dedicated to their advancement, and relentless in his pursuit of funding. His track record at the Olympics alone shows that we were right to appoint him to the job.*'

'What I meant by that,' says Jack, raising a hand in the air as if she's a buzzing fly that needs swatting away, 'was that on a purely professional level, if you look solely at the results he achieved, we appointed the right man.'

A murmur of dismay emerges across the aisles – even those who are, by their nature, supportive of middle-aged men and dismissive of young women find this remark problematic – and he raises his voice to be heard.

'No, listen now,' he says, waving a pudgy hand in the air. 'Yes, we got it badly wrong in some ways. We believed Mr Carvin to be a man of honour. Sure, there was nothing to suggest otherwise. But if you take the emotion out of the story and just separate the man and the job from what we subsequently learned, there's no one can deny his success in the role.'

'True enough,' says a man in the second row.

'How many medals did we win, after all, at the Olympics during his tenure? The world is a complicated place, Missy,' he continues, pointing his finger at his inquisitor. 'You'll find that out as you get a bit older and—'

'Don't patronize the girl!' shouts a woman from the back of the church, and half the audience bursts into applause while the other half, the male half, folds its arms. What is it, I wonder, about sporting success that seems more important to these men than basic decency?

'Look, I don't think any of us want to get bogged down in talking about Brendan Carvin,' says Jack, clearly eager for us to leave this conversation behind us. 'The man is where he ought to be, in the Midlands Prison, and there he will stay for the foreseeable future. And rest assured there will be more stringent safeguards put in place in the future to prevent something like this from ever happening again. If re-elected to Dáil Éireann, I will make it my personal responsibility to—'

And then, abruptly, he stops talking. I look up and realize that he is staring directly at me. In the moment, he's not entirely sure that I am who he thinks I am. My eyes meet his and I shake my head almost imperceptibly, beseeching him not to identify me. He continues to look, perhaps trying to understand what's happening here – is it me? If it is, where have I come from? And what do I want? – then, troubled, uncertain what to do, returns to what he was saying.

'I will make it my personal responsibility to make sure that nothing like that ever happens again,' he continues, quieter now, his confidence and bonhomie noticeably diminished. 'This country has a long and shameful history of people using their authority to destroy the lives of young people, and we cannot allow that to continue. My colleagues and I will put an end to the Brendan Carvins of this world.' He pauses and looks at me, as if to suggest that I am the villain of this story. 'And we will put an end to their enablers too. Those people who knew what was going on and looked away. In my book, complicity is just as bad as the crime itself.'

This goes down well and there's a sustained round of applause. I can't imagine that Lucy is satisfied with the response, for, after all, he is disassociating himself from the very crimes that he helped facilitate, while claiming credit for the medals that Ireland won. But the meeting is called to an end now and the audience rises to its feet, eager for their pints. I brush past the other people in my row, determined to get out quickly, and make my way down the nave towards the front doors. Pushing them open, I can't help myself. I glance back for a moment, and I see Jack taking selfies with some of the voters, a broad smile on his face. Perhaps he knows I'm watching because he looks down at me and the expression on his face changes immediately.

Don't you fucking judge me, it says. *Not you, of all people.*

12

On the day the police showed up at our front door, I was awake and dressed early, ready for a hair appointment booked for nine o'clock. The doorbell rang shortly before eight and, when I answered it, I was confronted by two Gardaí, one in plain clothes, who introduced herself as Sergeant Kilmartin, and the other in uniform. I froze when I saw them – it brought me immediately back to the day two of their colleagues had shown up at the hotel in Wexford – and my thoughts immediately turned to Rebecca, who had already left for college.

'What?' I said immediately, desperate for an answer to a question I hadn't even asked yet. 'Is it my daughter?'

'No, it's nothing like that,' said Sergeant Kilmartin, shaking her head quickly. 'Please don't worry, we're not here to deliver bad news.'

'Oh, thank God,' I replied, allowing myself to breathe again, but it only took a moment for me to wonder why, if that was not their purpose, then what was it?

'It's Mrs Carvin, isn't it?' she asked, and I nodded.

'That's right, yes.'

'Is your husband at home?'

'He's upstairs,' I said. 'Getting ready for work. Can I help you with something?'

'I'm afraid not, no. We need to speak to him. Do you mind if we come in?'

It was framed as a question, but in the moment I understood that I was not being given the option to refuse, and so I stood out of the way to allow them into the hallway. The senior officer looked tough and determined, while the junior appeared more apprehensive. From the kitchen, I heard the kettle turning off as it came to a boil and, a moment later, the toaster popping. Pointlessly, my mind drifted to a pot of jam I'd bought at a farmers' market a few days earlier that I'd intended on opening with my breakfast. Anything, perhaps, to stop myself from questioning why two officers might be standing before me. Stepping around them, I closed the front door and we stared at each other awkwardly until Garda Chen – his name was printed on his lapel – piped up.

'Perhaps you could call your husband down, Mrs Carvin,' he suggested, and I nodded before shouting up to Brendan, telling him there were some people here to see him. I heard him emerge from the bedroom, no doubt surprised that someone might be calling at such an hour, but he only made it halfway down the stairs before stopping. The moment he saw the Garda uniform, he visibly slumped against the bannister. That phrase one reads in books suggesting that the blood drains from a person's face when confronted by something horrific was proved wrong, for in Brendan's case, the opposite happened. Rather than paling, his cheeks grew inflamed, as if he had been surprised while committing some vulgar act and was mortified by his exposure.

'Mr Carvin,' said DS Kilmartin, looking up and introducing herself and her colleague, just as she had done to me. 'Could you come downstairs, please?'

Brendan took the rest of the stairs slowly, his head bowed.

'Mr Carvin,' she repeated when he was facing her, and she glanced quickly at her watch. 'It's 8.04 on the morning of March 23rd and I am placing you under arrest on the suspicion of sexually abusing a minor. You are not obliged to say anything unless you wish to do so, but whatever you say will be taken down in writing and may be given in evidence. Do you understand what I've just said?'

I looked, open-mouthed, from the two Gardaí to my husband and back again, before emitting something that sounded like an inappropriate laugh. I felt as if I was in a television drama, the words she had used being so familiar to me. Somehow, it surprised me that people actually employed them in real life.

'Brendan,' I said, turning to him now, but he wouldn't catch my eye. Instead, he continued to stare at the carpet, no doubt understanding immediately that, as of two minutes ago, the life that he had previously led had come to an end and that only ignominy and public disgrace lay before him. Before all of us.

DS Kilmartin turned to Garda Chen, nodded at him, and the young man stepped forward, producing a set of handcuffs, which he attached to Brendan's wrists, and my husband accepted them without a word of protest.

'Brendan,' I repeated, my voice rising now. 'Brendan, what's going on? What's happening here?'

'It's a mistake, Vanessa,' he muttered, shaking his head. 'A misunderstanding, that's all.'

And yet I knew that it wasn't, because if it was, he would be behaving with more outrage and surprise, rather than submitting himself in such a docile fashion.

'What is it you think he's done?' I asked, turning to DS Kilmartin, even though I had heard her words perfectly. 'Sexually abusing a minor? What minor? Who?'

'Mrs Carvin, I'm sorry, but I'm not at liberty to reveal that information to you,' she replied, not sounding sorry in the slightest.

'But you can't just—'

'We need to take your husband to the station now for questioning. You're welcome to follow if you wish, but I'm afraid you'll have to remain in reception, which doesn't have many facilities, and I expect your wait will be rather a long one, so I'd advise against. I imagine that Mr Carvin will be detained for most of today as we continue our inquiries.' She nodded towards Garda Chen once more and he promptly opened the front door and walked out, preceding Brendan, who trailed him like a dog, content to be led on his walk. The detective sergeant followed, while I stood in the doorway, blinking in the early-morning sunlight, bewildered by what had just taken place. As they put my husband into the back seat of their car, the postman wandered up the drive and handed me a letter, looking from me to the departing vehicle in curiosity. I glanced down at the envelope in my hand and could feel through the paper that it contained my new debit card, which I'd been expecting for the last few days. Uncertain what else to do, I returned inside, removed my old one from my purse, cut it up with the kitchen scissors and replaced it with the new before sitting down and replaying the entire scene in my head.

I'm not sure how long I sat there, trying to process it all, but I suspect it was quite some time. I only snapped out of my daze when my mobile phone, which was sitting on the table before me, rang. I picked it up and looked at the screen. An unfamiliar number came up but no name and, thinking that it might be someone from the Garda station, apologizing for what they'd done and inviting me to collect my husband and bring him home, I answered it.

'Mrs Carvin?' said a voice on the other end.

'Yes?'

'Richie Howling here, sports correspondent from the *Irish Times*. Do you have a moment to talk?'

I frowned. Why on earth was a reporter from the *Irish Times* calling me? How had he even got my number?

'Not really,' I said. 'What is it you want?'

'We've received a report that Brendan's been arrested on suspicion of abusing some of the young girls in his care at the National Swimming Federation. Do you have any comment to make?'

I held the phone away from my face and stared at it as if it was my mortal enemy, before trying to locate the button to end the call, but my vision had grown blurry now, and I couldn't seem to find it.

'Mrs Carvin?' he continued, his voice echoing through the empty room. 'Mrs Carvin, are you there? This is obviously going to be a major news story and I thought it might be helpful for you to get out front of it all and—'

I managed to hang up then, before throwing the phone away from me, like a hot coal or a grenade.

The rest of the day went by in free fall. Feeling that it would be a mistake to drive, I walked to the Garda station on Terenure Road West, where, as promised, I was left sitting in a stark waiting room with posters on the wall relating to domestic violence, cyber-security and lost dogs. To their credit, the Gardaí on duty, recognizing my confusion and distress, displayed some sympathy towards me, keeping me going with mugs of hot tea while expressing regret that they couldn't answer any of my questions. Finally, almost eight hours since she'd shown up at my front door, DS Kilmartin appeared to inform me that Brendan would not be permitted to return home that evening but would be held in the cells overnight before further questioning the following morning.

'But it can't be true,' I said, beseeching her to explain to me how something like this could happen. 'Brendan would never . . .' I found the words were lost in my throat. 'Who would say such a terrible thing about him?'

'I'm sorry, but I can't tell you that.'

'Well, whoever it is must be mad in the head.'

'We're investigating, Mrs Carvin. That's our job.'

'But you can't keep him here on the word of a disturbed child!' I protested.

'Actually, over the course of the day, more than one

complainant has come forward,' she told me in a tone that seemed rather pleased to be able to pass on this information.

'How many?' I asked, disbelieving.

'Two more. So far.'

It would be eight, of course, by the time the case came to court, and these were only the eight who chose to make their voices heard.

'But that's not my husband,' I protested. 'It's not. He's . . . he's a father . . . he's—'

'That's what we need to determine,' she interrupted, glancing at her watch, and I hated her for the contempt she was showing me. She seemed tired and, unlike her colleagues, unwilling to dispense any compassion towards me. She didn't accept my incredulity, and this was a sensation I would grow accustomed to over the year ahead. The feeling so many people had that if he was guilty, then I must have known about it all along.

'Has he admitted anything?' I asked.

'Not at all,' she replied, with a snort of a laugh. 'He claims he's innocent.'

'Well, then,' I said, as if that brought the matter to a close. 'What more do you need?'

'I'd advise you to go home,' she said. 'I won't have any more information for you tonight.'

I tried to protest, but she wouldn't be persuaded and, eventually, I had no choice but to leave. When I opened the doors of the station and stepped out on to the street, I was astonished to see a scrum of news reporters and photographers standing there. I glanced behind me, wondering who they were waiting for, but then the flashbulbs went off. When they started shouting my name, I realized they were waiting for me. I couldn't reply to their questions because the whole scene was simply too brutal and terrifying for any words. Instead, I threw myself into their centre, pushing forward and forcing them to make way for me, before practically flinging myself into the road in front of a passing taxi that had its lights on, and, fortunately, it stopped for me.

When I arrived home, Rebecca was sitting in the dark in the living room. I turned the lights on, and we stared at each other for a long time. Her expression was entirely unsympathetic.

'Did you know?' she asked, and I shook my head.

'Of course not,' I said. 'How could I have? It's not true anyway. It can't be true. And who told you?'

'It's all over the fucking news!' she roared, frightening me with her anger. 'A friend pulled me out of a lecture to show me what people were saying on Twitter.'

And then she stood up and approached me and, for the first time, I realized that she had grown to a height where we could look each other directly in the eye.

'Emma,' she said.

I frowned, wondering why she was changing the subject.

'What about Emma?' I asked.

'Emma,' she repeated, and, finally, I lost my composure for the first time that day.

'What?' I screamed, spittle flying in my daughter's

face. 'What about Emma? What are you talking about, you silly girl?'

And now I felt the room begin to swim, and I might have collapsed had Rebecca not reached out to steady me. It had been half a day since the doorbell had rung, and this had never crossed my mind.

'No,' I said, my voice low as I shook my head, unwilling to concede for even a moment that what she was suggesting might be possible. 'No, he didn't. He wouldn't. He couldn't. No, you're wrong. He'd never do such a thing to his own daughter. He loved her. Why would you say such a thing? What's wrong with you? What in God's name is wrong with you?'

13

When the storm comes, I am frightened. It streaks across the island like a banshee, and Bananas raises himself in the armchair, his claws gripping the frayed wool, turning to glare at me as if he holds me responsible for the weather. I cannot get out for two days because the rain and wind are so strong that there's a chance I might not even make it to the village in one piece, although I long to be in the warmth of either pub with the consolation of other voices around me. I am careful with the food in the fridge, rationing my provisions as people must have done in Famine days.

When the squall hurls itself against the windows, I wonder how they don't concede defeat and shatter inwards, shredding me in the process. Even the roof seems as if it's only clinging on to the masonry out of good manners. But who was it who told me that Peadar Dooley's cottage had been built from good bricks? Whoever it was, he was right.

Bananas is mewling at the door now, scraping his nails against it, and although I caution him that there is nothing but danger outside, he seems desperate to leave. As comfortable as he is here, it seems that he would, inexplicably, prefer to be with that scourge Mrs Duggan. When I open the door, he flings himself outside, where the rain falls in sheets and, in a moment, he has vanished from sight altogether. I call his name, beseeching him to return, but he's a braver soul than I and is surely running as fast as he can towards home. Perhaps he would like to be wrapped up safely in Luke's arms, a sentiment to which I can relate.

I remain in the doorway for a few moments, taking in the extraordinary sights and sounds that greet me, warning me from going any further. This is how I had imagined the island would be when I first studied it on a map and considered it for my exile. Torrential rain. Inhabitants crouched in their houses, waiting for the eternal tempest to soften. The fear of what might be happening to those on the water. I shout into the wind, eager to hear my voice, to confirm that I still have one, but it's lost in the gale, which howls back at me, impressed by my fortitude but demanding that I return inside. I draw the latch across the woodwork, throw some more logs on the fire, and collapse on the sofa, laughing a little. We never had weather like this in Dublin. It's an experience, if nothing else.

My phone rings and I'm greeted by an unfamiliar number. My first instinct is that someone from the village is calling to check on me. Ifechi, perhaps. I want to be rescued but I'm loath to have my solitude disturbed and am uncertain whether to answer. Curiosity takes hold of me, however, and, before it can ring out, I answer.

An automated voice tells me that a call has been placed

to me from Midlands Prison. If I am willing to accept it, I should press 'star' now. If I am not, I can simply hang up. Despite myself, I search for the 'star' and do as instructed.

He says my name. My real name. Vanessa.

'Brendan,' I reply, uncertain how to react. 'Is it you?'

'Who else would it be?'

'But how are you calling me?'

'We're allowed calls,' he tells me. 'I wanted to talk.'

I say nothing. In my head, I summon up images from American prison movies. Brendan standing at a payphone, one arm locked around it for privacy, while a group of impatient men stand behind him, ready to drag him away if he stays any longer than necessary. I wonder is what we see in films anything like real life. Probably not.

'Talk about what?' I ask, and I wish I had received some warning of this call, that he had not ambushed me in this way. There's been so many times when I've imagined the things I would say if I was confronted by him – I've paced the cottage holding make-believe conversations aloud – but they're all lost to me now with the surprise.

The last time we spoke was on the morning of his sentencing, when Rebecca and I arrived at the Four Courts and spotted him standing in a corner with his barrister. He came towards us both and while Rebecca turned on her heel and made her way quickly into the courtroom, I stood my ground while he told me that he was innocent, that the jury had made a mistake, that the whole thing was a kangaroo court, that the media had played a part in his conviction, that the girls who had accused him were filthy little things who'd shown an interest in him but he hadn't reciprocated, that nothing was more important to him than our marriage, that he loved me, that he needed me to tell the reporters outside what a sham all this was, that he'd never survive in prison, that the judge would surely overturn the verdict, that he might have to sue his barrister, that he'd take this to the European Court of Human Rights if he had to, that—

He said more, I daresay, but it was all to my back.

Now, however, he is silent. Even though he's the one who called me, he doesn't seem to know what he wants to say. I can't help myself. I fall into old ways and act the part of the dutiful wife.

'How are you getting on in there?' I ask, and I hear a deep sigh, followed by what sounds like a sob.

'It's not easy, love,' he says.

'It's not supposed to be.'

'I can't do twelve years of it.'

'You probably won't have to.'

Another long silence before he speaks again.

'How are things at home?' he asks, and I decide not to tell him that I have left Terenure, that our house is locked up for now.

'Quiet,' I tell him.

'Are the neighbours giving you a hard time?'

'Not too bad,' I say, even though most of them ignored me from the moment Brendan's actions made the papers. People I'd known for decades. People I considered friends.

'I'm thinking of taking a holiday,' I say, inventing this out of thin air.

'What?' he asks, surprised. 'Where to?'

I search my brain for destinations far away. 'Sydney, Australia,' I tell him. 'I've never been.'

'And how will you pay for that?'

I frown. It can't be that big a mystery to him. 'From our savings,' I say.

'Don't be digging into that too much,' he says. 'I'll need that for the appeal.'

'You can't waste money on that,' I say.

'Why not?'

'Because it won't change the verdict.'

I feel rather brave speaking to him in this way. I'm not sure I would have the courage if he was standing in front of me.

'The truth will out,' he insists.

'It already did.'

'No, it didn't,' he snaps. 'They've put me in here to cover their own backs. It's a conspiracy, sure a blind man could see that.'

I sigh. I really don't want to hear any more of his self-justifications or his lies.

'Have you made any friends at least?' I ask.

'You're joking, aren't you? Sure there's rapists and murderers and all sorts in here.'

'But you're a rapist,' I say calmly. 'And you have blood on your hands.'

'I can't make friends with the likes of them,' he

continues, ignoring this. 'I don't have a fair shake of it on account of what they all think I did.'

'But you did do those things, Brendan,' I point out. 'And more besides, I daresay.'

'I didn't,' he insists, raising his voice. 'Sure what do you take me for?'

'But you did,' I repeat. 'And at some point you'll have to face up to it and admit what you did. You're a guilty man.'

A pause.

'You always thought the worst of me.'

'Brendan,' I say, and again my tone remains composed, despite the words that tumble from my mouth. 'It's not just about the eight girls you abused, the eight that came forward, I mean. It's also about Emma. You abused her, you terrible man. You violated her. I don't know how long it went on for. I don't know how many times you did it. She tried to tell me once, you know, and I didn't listen. I should be in that prison alongside you for not listening. I am, in a sense, although there are no locked doors.' I recognize the irony of my words, for all Emma ever asked of me was for a locked door and I denied her it. 'You raped our daughter, Brendan. You raped her. Don't you see that? Will you not acknowledge it at least, out of respect for her memory? And she killed herself because of it. She swam out as far as she could one dark night on Curracloe Beach, to a point where she knew there would be no way back. Do you ever wonder what went through her mind at that moment, when all was lost? Did she panic? Did she feel regret? Or was it relief, because she knew you couldn't get your filthy hands on her ever again. Does that not keep you awake at night, Brendan? Because it does me. Our job was to protect her, to protect both of them. Nothing else. But what I didn't know when I married you was that you were a man of no conscience or moral character. Quite honestly, my preference would be that you die in prison. That's the call I want to receive from Midlands Prison. From the governor. Telling me that you're in a box. Not this nonsense from you, pleading innocence and talking about appeals.'

I almost can't believe that I've managed to say all this without stumbling over my words or having him interrupt, but there's so much relief in having said them at last. When he eventually replies, his tone is hard and vicious.

'You're as brainwashed as the rest of them,' he tells me. 'You lived off for me for thirty years, you filthy bitch, and when I'm laid low, when I need you more than—'

I don't hear the end of that sentence as I've already hung up. I'm trembling. I stare at the phone in my hand, as if it has betrayed me in some way. I picture my husband shouting 'Hello? hello?' into the receiver and someone behind him telling him that his time's up and to fuck off out of it, and Brendan simpering before him like the coward he is before running back to his cell with his head down. Should this image satisfy me? Because it doesn't. I can take no pleasure in it whatsoever.

I open one of the cupboards and extract the bottle of whiskey, pour myself a healthy glass, and drink it down in one go. The phone sits on the counter now and I pick it up, opening the text application to see the face of my remaining child.

She has changed her picture again. Now it shows her and Emma in their teenage years, arms around each other, laughing uproariously. I've never seen this one before, so I take a screenshot and save it to my gallery before she can change it again.

Your father phoned me, I write and, a few moments later, to my astonishment, a reply appears.

There is no such person.

I nod and put the phone away.

Outside, the storm is worse than ever. How can the island even retain its foundation in the earth? How is it not dragged from its mooring and hurtled into the sky, spinning away into the clouds like Dorothy's house? I pull on my raincoat. I need fresh air. I need to feel the wind and the rain on my face in order to wash away the obscenity of that call. I open the latch, then the door, and it bursts outwards in ecstasy, like a body emerging from a near-drowning, reaching the surface and gasping for air.

I don't quite know where I'm going, and it's difficult to see anyway, but I make my way in the general direction of the seafront and start singing at the top of my voice. An old song. 'The Shoals of Herring'. I'm no great singer, but it doesn't matter. These are shouts more than anything else. I'm roaring into the wind about fishing the Swarth and the Broken Bank, sailing towards Canny Shiels with a hundred cran of silver darlings, and oh, if anyone was to hear me now, they would think Willow Hale, the woman who came from Dublin without a husband and took up residence in Peadar Dooley's cottage, and talked to islanders, and had her lunch every day in the old pub, and slept with Luke Duggan, has gone off her mind from loneliness and will now be known as the Madwoman of the Upper Hills. But no one can hear me, for I am as alone here as I have ever been in my life. I stretch my arms wide and throw my head back, opening my mouth to capture the rainwater, and how is it possible, I ask myself, to feel so at peace in such chaos?

In the distance, on the Duggan farm, I think I see Luke staring down at me, as he did the first time I saw him, but he would be as foolish as me to venture out into this bedlam, so perhaps I'm imagining things. I daresay that mother of his would drag him back in by the scruff of the neck anyway, promising him pneumonia if he stays outside another minute. I blink, my eyes finding it difficult to focus, and maybe he is there and maybe he isn't, and what matter either way, because I can't get that line out of my head, it's repeating over and over –

You lived off for me for thirty years, you filthy bitch, and when I'm laid low . . . You lived off for me for thirty years, you filthy bitch, and when I'm laid low . . . You lived off for me for thirty years, you filthy bitch, and when I'm laid low . . .

And I weep at the loss of everything that was once mine. The loss of Emma. The loss of Rebecca. And, may God forgive me, the loss of Brendan too, who I loved once, before struggling back towards the cottage. The wind is against me and every step takes effort and there is a part of me that wants to lay down on the grass and let it do its worst. How long would I survive? An hour, perhaps? A little more? The elements – water, earth, fire, air – are our greatest friends, our animators. They feed us, warm us, give us life, and yet conspire to kill us at every juncture. But I don't need their permission to take me away. If I could simply clap my hands and fall into a deep sleep out here, never to wake again, I would clap them. I would clap them again and again and again until I was gone from this world and reborn or forgotten, whatever the universe decided.

The door is in sight now and I trip over what I think might be a rock, falling to the ground, my hands splayed out before me. Grizzly pebbles crush into my palms, tearing at them, drawing blood, stigmata on my skin, and I lie there, sodden, the storm doing its best to finish me off. I am howling at the pain and misfortune of my life, and when I turn to curse the stone that felled me, I see that it was no stone at all, it was Bananas the cat, for he would not take my advice and stay indoors, and the weather has done for him. In that moment, I weep for this miserable, aggressive feline who somehow came to be my companion, but I envy him too.

'You're better off out of it, my love,' I say, but the wind lifts my words away, and what does it matter anyway when he's past hearing them.

14

AND NOW, HERE SHE IS.

In my cottage. Unannounced. Unexpected. Uninvited. But welcome, always welcome.

My child. My daughter. My survivor.

Rebecca.

'How did you find me?' I ask her, sitting down on the sofa and placing my hands between my knees, for they are noticeably trembling. I feel that I should maintain some distance between us in case I suffocate her with too much affection and she takes fright and runs away. It's the afternoon before wash day and I'm in my rags. I don't know if this will count for or against me. Maybe she'll think I've let myself go since leaving Dublin. I don't want her to think that Brendan has somehow weakened me; he hasn't. If anything, after all this time, I've found strength here. Without him.

'You told me where you were,' she replies, and I shake my head.

'No, I meant the cottage,' I say. 'Not the island.'

'Oh, I went into the pub when I got off the boat,' she tells me. 'I asked about you there.'

'And they told you?'

'Yes.'

I frown. How is this possible? Everyone here knows me as Willow Hale. But Rebecca knows me as Vanessa Carlin.

'It was weird,' she continues, glancing around, taking the place in. 'All I had to say was, I'm looking for my mother, and the man behind the bar knew who I was immediately. He said I was the spit of you.'

I smile. People always said that Emma was the one who took after me; it's nice to know that I might have passed on something to Rebecca too.

'I don't think we're anything alike, though,' she adds, bursting my bubble.

'Why didn't you let me know that you were coming?' I ask.

'I wasn't sure if I was really going to or not and didn't want to say I would and then disappoint you. Even when I arrived on the island, I thought about turning back.'

'Why?'

In reply, she simply sniffs the air, as if she's caught a scent of something distasteful.

'Do you have a dog?' she asks. 'Is there a dog here somewhere?'

'A cat,' I tell her. 'Well, it wasn't mine. It just liked to visit. It used to sit where you're sitting, that's probably the scent you're getting. Then it went out in a storm and didn't make it home. I miss it, even though neither of us ever showed the slightest affection for the other.'

'You miss the cat,' she says, and I can't tell whether this is a question or a statement of fact. Perhaps she's thinking it through in her mind. Her mother is here alone, she's lost a daughter, her husband is in prison, her other daughter barely speaks to her. And she misses a cat.

'It's good to see you,' I tell her.

'And you,' she says, relenting a little. 'I've missed you.'

I nod but don't repeat the words back to her. I have to play this very carefully if I'm not to scare her away.

'And how are you?' I ask, thinking that small talk is a good place to start.

'Better than I was. But not as good as I could be. And you?'

'The same, I think.'

'You like it here?'

'I don't dislike it.'

'You never told me why.'

'Why what?'

'Why this island?'

'Oh,' I say, laughing. 'I probably never told you this, but I came here once before. Years ago, when I was just a girl. Fifteen years old, I think. It's a Gaeltacht area during the summer and six of us from school arrived for three weeks after our Inter Cert, supposedly to improve our Irish. It's so long ago I can't remember much about the place other than the fact that I enjoyed it. It was the first time I got away from your grandparents, you see, so it was a chance for a bit of independence. After the trial, when I knew I needed to escape Dublin, I considered London, but thought that would have been too busy. Then I wondered whether I might go to America. But the States would have been too far.'

'From home?'

'No, sweetheart, from you. So then I thought . . . here.'

Rebecca smiles. 'First kiss?' she asks, and I laugh, delighted that she wants to tease me. This is the relationship I want to have with my daughter. One where we can laugh and share, like adults.

'It was, actually,' I say. 'Everyone back then had their first kiss in the Gaeltacht.'

'What was his name?'

'Oh, for heaven's sake, I can't remember! It was so long ago. Although I remember he had a mullet and looked like one of Echo and the Bunnymen.'

'Who?'

'They were a band. Colin liked them.'

'Who's Colin?'

'The boy I kissed.'

'You said you couldn't remember his name.'

I laugh and find my face bursting into a scarlet blush, which makes us both laugh. This is delightful. 'Fine,' I say. 'His name was Colin Marley and I was obsessed from the minute I laid eyes on him. He wore a leather jacket and, along with the mullet, he had beautiful blue eyes that looked at you as if he was a little confused why you, or he, were even alive in the world. He was from Westmeath, and when I got back home we wrote to each other for a couple of months, and swore that we'd meet up at Hallowe'en in Dublin, but then he wrote to tell me that he'd found a girlfriend in Athlone, and I cried for days.'

Rebecca looks overjoyed by this story. My mind drifts for a moment back to that boy, back to Colin. He sat next to me in Irish class on the island and sometimes I thought he was too beautiful even to turn my head to look at. As if he was some gorgeous Medusa who might turn me to stone if I so much as glanced in his direction.

'Your hair,' she says.

'Yes, I know.'

'It's so short.'

'It's convenient.'

'Actually, it looks good.'

'Do you think so?' I ask her. 'I did it myself with a pair of scissors. There's a woman below in the village who cuts hair in her kitchen, but I didn't want to bother her. She'd only end up yapping at me and asking me questions. Anyway, it was the first thing I did when I came to the island. No, the second.'

'What was the first?'

'It doesn't matter.'

I don't want to tell her that I've changed my name. She's still a Carvin, after all, and I don't want her to feel that I've placed more than just a geographical distance between us.

'Have you come to bring me home?' I ask after a lengthy pause, and she shakes her head.

'No,' she tells me. 'It's up to you where you live. And you've been here, how long is it now? Seven months?'

'Eight.'

'And you're not bored?'

'You'd be surprised how busy a person can keep when there's nothing to do. Every night, I make a full plan for the next day before I go to bed. I go for long walks. I talk to people in the village. And there's always a bit of drama to keep me occupied.' I hesitate for a moment, then decide to throw caution to the wind. 'Also, I have sex quite frequently, and that's been a godsend. I'd forgotten how good it can be if you're doing it with someone who knows what he's doing and wants you to enjoy it as much as he does.'

Her eyes open wide, and I can tell that she's not entirely sure she heard me correctly. I rather enjoy the fact that I've shocked her.

'What did you say?' she asks.

'I said I have sex quite frequently,' I repeat. 'It's nothing long term. A younger man.'

'What? How young?'

'Well, I was at his twenty-fifth birthday party in the old pub a few months back.'

'Twenty-five?' She looks astonished.

'Yes. A gentle soul. He was interested, so was I, so we both just went with it.'

'I see,' she says, and it's clear from her expression that she thinks I have taken leave of my senses. 'And is this a . . . is he a boyfriend now? Are you, like, dating?'

'Oh no,' I reply quickly. 'Not at all. But we've become good friends and the reason it works is that neither of us places any demands upon the other. Sometimes, if I'm in the mood, I text him. Sometimes, if he's in the mood, he texts me. Then he comes over, we have a drink and a chat and, when we've exhausted all our conversation, we go to bed together. He doesn't stay over. It's something we both take pleasure in. I like him, I think he likes me too. But if either of us ended it tomorrow, I'm sure that neither of us would give it another thought, and our lives would go on as before.'

'Right,' she says, and I can tell that she doesn't know how to process any of this. This is a conversation she never imagined having with me. I suspect she wants to place it somewhere in the corner of her mind and think about it, or not think about it, later.

'What's his name?' she asks.

'Luke.'

She nods.

'Luke what?'

'Luke Duggan.'

A silence.

'And what about you?' I ask. 'Are you seeing anyone?'

'No one special,' she says, as secretive as ever. 'So, is this it? Do you live here now? Are you never coming back to Dublin?'

'I will, sooner or later,' I tell her. 'Right now, I'm still taking it day by day.'

'What about the house?'

'What about it?'

'Are you going to sell it?'

'I hadn't given it any thought. Why, would you like it?'

'No,' she says quickly. 'No, I don't ever want to set foot in it again. But if you sold it—'

'If I sold it, I would give you half,' I say, and, making my mind up suddenly, I add: 'In fact, let's do that. I don't want to go back there either, so I'll get in touch with someone tomorrow and put it on the market and we'll split the proceeds fifty–fifty. How does that sound?'

She stares at me, as if she's uncertain whether she can allow herself to believe this spontaneous offer.

'Really?' she asks. 'You'd do that?'

'Of course I would. I've plenty of savings. And adding my half of the house into that will give me security for life. And your half will set you up nicely, won't it?'

'It will,' she says. 'But you should think about it. It's a lot of—'

'I have thought about it. I thought about it just now. The plan is made. There now.'

'And what about . . . him?' she asks. 'Won't he have some say in it?'

'Not a thing,' I tell her. 'Your grandad gave us the deposit for a wedding present but insisted on putting my name on the deeds. We always meant to change them but never got around to it. So I can do whatever the hell I want. I'll empty the joint account too and split that between the pair of us.'

'Then what will he do for money when he gets out?'

'He can live on the streets, for all I care. Do you care? If you do, tell me now, and I'll split it three ways.'

She thinks about it. 'No,' she says. 'No, I don't. But maybe we could take his third and—'

She makes a suggestion for what to do with Brendan's share and it tells me what a marvellous young woman she is. She wants to help others. Girls like those who my husband, her father, has destroyed. I agree immediately.

'Thank you,' she says. 'I wasn't asking so you'd say something like that. But my share will give me options.'

'Just use it wisely, that's all I ask.'

Always the mother.

She smiles.

I feel I have done something good for her at last.

Another lengthy pause. I can sense this question is coming. He's still her father, after all.

'Have you spoken to him?' she asks.

'Just the once,' I tell her. 'But we didn't talk for long.'

'What did he want?'

'To tell me how miserable he was. And how innocent he was. And what a terrible wife I was.'

'Fuck him,' she says, and it shocks me a little to hear my daughter use this language. It would never have been allowed when she was growing up. But:

'I couldn't agree more,' I tell her.

'I hate him.'

'I know.'

'Sometimes, I've hated you too.'

'There'd be something wrong with you if you hadn't.'

'Why did you let it happen?'

'I didn't,' I protest. 'If I had known—'

'If you had known what?'

'About those poor girls.'

'And Emma?'

Mentioning her name is like pressing a sharp knife deep into my heart. The pain of it.

'I don't know,' I whisper, looking down at the floor, for I cannot look her in the eyes. 'I came here to find out whether I was—'

'What?'

'Complicit,' I say.

'And?'

'I don't know,' I tell her truthfully. 'Maybe I'll never be able to answer that question. I've tried, God knows I've tried, but I think I'm condemned to ask it of myself every hour of every day until I breathe my last. I tried to be a good mother.' To my surprise, I realize that tears are running down my cheeks. I wipe them away – both hands, it takes – but they continue to fall. 'Truly, I did. Perhaps I wasn't cut out for it, but I did my best. I loved you both. You were my daughters. Nothing mattered more.'

'I know,' she says.

'I would die for you, Rebecca, do you realize that? I would throw myself under a speeding train if it kept you safe. And I would die to bring Emma back to life.'

'She never told you? What he did to her? You promise me?'

'I swear it on my life,' I say.

A lengthy pause. She waits. I bow my head. I feel my body collapse into itself. I must be honest. If I'm not, then how can we ever be what we should be to each other?

'Once, she asked me to put a lock on her bedroom door,' I tell her. 'I didn't like the idea of it, so I said no. It was . . . it was a mistake.'

'Did you know why she was asking?'

I want to throw my head back and scream at the moon.

'I don't know,' I tell her. 'I can't put myself back in that moment.'

And now I am weeping.

'I don't know if I guessed and chose to do nothing, or

if it didn't cross my mind at all. I don't know. I don't, I swear it. If she had told me and I'd accused her of lying, or just ignored it, then I would have been a monster. But never even to notice? Never even to suspect? That's what shames me the most. That's what makes me question myself. Was I blind, or just stupid?'

She's crying now too but she shakes her head. She cannot answer this question for me. Neither of us can.

I stand up and make my way towards the sink for some kitchen roll to wipe my eyes dry. 'That is what haunts me more than anything else,' I tell her. 'I don't know if I knew or not. I don't know. One makes me blind, but the other makes me inhuman. Either way, I don't come out of it well.'

I stare at her. She is looking down at the floor. I've never known her to cry so much for she's never been an emotional person, not even when she was a child. Even when Emma died, she was more brittle than demonstrative in her grief. At the funeral, she simply stared ahead and refused to speak to anyone.

'What?' I ask her. 'What's wrong?'

'You can't guess?' she asks, looking up at me.

'No. What is it?'

She breathes heavily, as if she has just finished running a race, before putting her head in her hands.

'She told me,' she says in a low voice. 'The night before she died, she told me. We were on holiday, remember?'

I nod but say nothing. Of course I remember.

'She told me that night in the hotel bedroom. She told me what he did to her. What he'd been doing to her for years. She told me because she didn't want him to do it to me. And I called her a liar. I said it wasn't true, that she was only saying it for attention, because he never touched me. I said some terrible things to her. She begged me to believe her, but I wouldn't. I threw her out of the room. I told her that I didn't care where she slept, but that she wasn't sharing that room with me. I locked the door. I went to bed. And, in the morning, she was gone. So, you see, I blame you but it's really my fault. If I had just listened to her, if I had believed her . . .'

I'm in shock. There's a part of me that wants to slap her across the face, to drag her to the floor and kick her until she curls up into a ball. And there's another part that wants to wrap her up in my arms and tell her that we are none of us innocent and none of us guilty, and we all have to live with what we've done for the rest of our lives and that the only way through this terrible thing, if we are to survive it at all, is to be kind to each other and to love one another.

Instead, I tell her that I need a moment on my own and retire to the bathroom, locking the door behind me, and stare at myself in the mirror.

'My life,' I whisper under my breath. 'What has become of my life?'

When I finally emerge, she is standing by the window, and, to my astonishment, she has taken the kitchen scissors and cut her hair to match my own. Her long tendrils are on the floor around her feet.

'We're the same now,' she says. 'As bad as each other.'

'The Carvin women,' I say, shaking my head sadly.

'No,' she replies. 'Not me. Not any more.'

I frown, uncertain what she means.

'I changed my name. Well, my surname, at least.'

'When?'

'The day you left. Well, later that day, actually. Probably when you arrived here.'

I remain silent for a moment.

'To what?' I ask.

'I didn't have many options. I could invent a new one or choose yours. Your maiden name, I mean. So that's what I did.'

'Hale,' I say.

'Hale,' she agrees.

I feel a flood of love wash over me. I don't bother to tell her that I did the same thing at the same time. I will, some day. But not just yet. It is wonderful. It is right. We are no longer Carvins, either of us. We are no longer his.

I step towards her. I place my hands on her shoulders and lean forward, and she does the same. Our foreheads meet and we close our eyes. If it were possible, I would stay in this position for ever. Between us lingers the presence of another. It is Emma. We three are here together, a mother and her daughters. He, that man, is absent. He is no longer part of us. He is a demon, exorcized. Emma pulls us together, restful, serene, wrapping her arms around us, happy to see the two people she loved the most are at peace with each other.

Or are at the beginnings of a peace anyway, which is almost the same thing.

15

TODAY, I LEAVE THE island.

I pack my suitcase and, although I've bought no new clothes or souvenirs during my stay here, it seems fuller than when I arrived. Walking around the few small rooms that have been my home this last year, I make sure that I have left nothing behind me, before writing a note for Peadar Dooley, whoever he might be, thanking him for allowing me to rent his cottage, and placing it on the table.

As I stand in the centre of the living room, I wonder how much I have changed in the time that I've spent here. I feel more at peace, certainly. When I first took the train from Dublin to Galway, and then the ferry across to the island, I was frightened of discovery; now, I'm less concerned, as the media has inevitably moved on since Brendan is more than a year into his sentence. I daresay there have been other scandals in the meantime, scandals to which I am oblivious. Other women fleeing the misdeeds of the men they trusted.

When I hear the sound of a car pulling up outside, I assume it is Mícheál Óg Ó'Ceallaigh, who I have asked to collect me, and I feel only a small sentimental sadness as I lock the door behind me, placing the key under the flowerpot as instructed, and make my way towards him. Only, to my surprise, it is not Mícheál Óg sitting behind the wheel, it is Luke.

'I cancelled your taxi,' he tells me when I open the door. 'You don't mind, do you? I thought you might prefer a friendlier face on your last morning. Mícheál Óg's would curdle milk.'

I smile and feel an enormous sense of gratitude towards him. We said our goodbyes already, two nights ago, but what harm to say them again.

'Thank you,' I say, settling into the passenger seat and buckling the belt as he drives over the gravel and down the makeshift road. 'This is very good of you.'

How lucky I was to have met him! We were a mutual convenience that worked out splendidly. We never bothered to discuss what our relationship is, or was, or might have been. We just enjoyed every minute of it.

'I hear he's already got it rented again,' says Luke as we drive along. 'Peadar, I mean.'

'The cottage?'

'Sure enough. The rumour is that it's some actress escaping Hollywood after a break-up with her fella.'

'Good Lord. And I suppose you'll head over to say hello?' I ask, teasing him, and he laughs, even blushes a little.

'Well, it's good to be neighbourly, isn't it?' He turns to smile at me, then we both dissolve in silly giggles. I adore him and want nothing from him. We want nothing from each other. Which was why what we shared was perfect.
'So, what's next for you?' he asks, and I shrug my shoulders, for I've been asking myself the same question over

the last two weeks, since I decided it was time to leave, and I still haven't arrived at a satisfactory answer.

'I have to pack up the house,' I tell him. 'It went sale agreed a few days ago so I'll box up the things I want to hold on to and get a man with a van to take what's left to the charity shop. After that, I need to find somewhere to live. And, I thought, get a job.'

'What sort of a job?'

'Whatever will keep me busy. The thing is, Luke, I've never worked. And I'm only fifty-three. I want to be out and among people. To have some fun. I haven't had much fun in my life. It never seemed like a priority. I feel ready to change that. We had fun, didn't we?'

'Plenty of it.'

'And I'd like some more.'

'So you'll stay in Dublin?'

'Probably,' I tell him. 'But who knows? You're welcome to visit if you want,' I add tentatively, and he turns to me and smiles, as if to suggest that he's grateful for the offer but no, that's not something he'll be doing. I'm not sure that I'd even want him to. He wouldn't belong there any more than I ever belonged here.

'You'll be fine,' he says, and, as on the first night we met, when he first advised me to be careful of the water, there's nothing patronizing in his tone.

'And you?' I ask. 'You'll stay here?'

'I will,' he admits. 'Sure, I'm too old to move now.'

'Luke, you're twenty-five,' I say, rolling my eyes at such defeatism. 'You have your entire life in front of you.'

'I know, but, well, I'm happy enough here. I fit in.' He

nods in the general direction of the bigger island that gives us our identity. 'I'd be a fish out of water beyond.'

We pull into the dock and he places the car in neutral, pulls up the handbrake, and takes my right hand in his left, before lifting it to his mouth, kissing it gently, and releasing it.

'Right then, Willow Hale,' he says. 'Shall we get moving?'

We climb out of the car and, as he retrieves my suitcase from the boot, I notice Ifechi standing by the platform that leads to the waiting boat. It's not the regular ferry, but a smaller one that can be specially booked when you need to travel outside of the scheduled hours. I smile in his direction. I'm glad he came to see me off.

'I didn't make a convert out of you,' he says when I approach him, and we shake hands, somehow nervous of hugging.

'I'm afraid not,' I reply. 'But you did your best and that's what counts.'

'Will you come back to see us again?'

Luke places the suitcase on the ground next to me and looks up, interested in the answer to this question.

'I don't think so,' I say. 'I must put all of this behind me now.'

'But you won't forget us?'

'Oh no,' I say, extending the handle of the suitcase and shaking my head. 'No, I won't forget you. Any of you. Goodbye, Ifechi.'

Two kisses, one for him and one for Luke, and that's it. I make my way along the platform and a man I don't recognize helps me on board, taking my suitcase and placing it in the rear, in the centre, for balance. Then, as I am the only passenger, he starts the engine, but, before he can leave, a voice from the dock stops him. I look around and it's Evan Keogh, the boy who took his father's boat out and almost didn't come back. He's running towards us, his mother a few steps behind, a rucksack slung over his shoulder.

'Are you joining us, Maggie?' shouts the sailor, and she shakes her head.

'Not me,' she calls back. 'Just Evan.'

Mother and son are locked in conversation now and I see her putting a bundle of banknotes into his hand, folding his fingers around them. She pulls him towards her, tight, as if she might never see him again, then pushes him away.

'Go on now,' she says, her voice filled with urgency, as if they're being chased. 'Go on now, you, and don't look back.'

And he follows her instructions, throwing his bag into the boat and leaping in.

'Right so,' says our captain, and, a moment later, the boat pulls away, its stern pointed in the direction of Galway. I watch Maggie Keogh – her expression blends sorrow and relief – until she has disappeared from view.

'You're leaving, then?' I ask, turning to Evan, who startles a little, as if surprised to be spoken to.

'I am,' he tells me.

'Tell me to mind my own business if you want, but am I right in thinking you're a great footballer?'

'That's what they tell me,' he says. 'But I have no more interest in it than I do in the man in the moon.'

I'm surprised by his response. I understood that most teenage boys longed for a life in sport. Clearly, he's different.

'And where are you going?' I ask.

He smiles. The weather is perfect for this voyage, and we make easy companions.

'England, to begin with,' he tells me.

'And what's in England?' I ask.

'My future. And you?'

'Dublin.'

'And what's in Dublin?'

'My past.'

'Then leave it there,' he says, and I'm surprised to hear such sensible advice from a boy who can't be more than seventeen.

'What do you suggest?' I ask.

'Go somewhere no one knows you. Start again. I know who you are, by the way. And who your husband was. I never told anyone, but I always knew. I've seen you around.'

'And I've seen you around.'

'I was a bit intrigued.'

I laugh. It's an unusual phrase for a boy his age.

'Were you indeed?' I say.

'Yes,' he replies.

'Well, thank you for keeping it to yourself.'

He nods and looks out at the water. We are safe from it in this sturdy little boat, but I will be happier when we reach Galway.

'Did the island give you whatever you needed?' he asks me after a while, and I have to think about this, because I want to give him an honest answer.

'I think it did,' I tell him. 'Now, I just have to figure out how to use its gifts.'

'Don't go to Dublin,' he says.

'Why not?'

'Because it's small. And the world is big. Fuck Dublin,' he adds. He seems so excited to be on this boat. He is breathless for the life he's entering into and I hope that he will not know pain or betrayal or disappointment, but of course he will, because he's alive and that's the price we pay.

We say nothing for a while, occasionally looking across at each other and smiling, but feeling no need to continue with our conversation. Might you have been Zac, I wonder, imagining my ghost-child, the one who might have saved us all, since the living proved so hopeless.

'Do you know anyone in England?' I ask him in time.

'Not a soul.'

'And you're not frightened?'

When he smiles, his whole face lights up. He is the very sunshine.

'Not a bit of it,' he says. 'I'm excited. Do you know the first thing I'm going to do when I get there?'

'What?' I ask.

'Change my name.'

The three of us – the sailor, the boy, and I – remain silent for the final part of our voyage. The sailor is probably thinking about what he'll have for his dinner when he turns around, having dropped us off and made his way home. The boy is looking towards the mainland, anticipating everything to come. And me, well, I intend to get riotously drunk in the pubs around Eyre Square tonight, on my own, and I will call this the end of the first half of my life. Tomorrow, I will wake up and begin again.

Soon, lights start to twinkle in the distance, through the mist, and I can hear the sounds of life on the approaching shore. It's only another island that I'm approaching, of course, a larger one than the one on which I've spent this last year, but it holds the body of my elder daughter in its earth, the worthless bones of my husband in one of its prisons, and the beautiful spirit of my younger daughter in its capital. And, in a few minutes, it will reclaim me.

Willow Hale.

Vanessa Carvin.

Whatever name I choose.

I can be any woman in Ireland.

The engine dies and the boat drifts towards the shore.

The sailor throws out a rope to a man waiting on the dock and he ties it quickly around a mooring post. I'm gathering my things together as Evan makes his way nimbly off the boat, puts his rucksack down and, a gentleman to his core, reaches out a hand to take my suitcase from me, but I wave it away.

'No, you're grand,' I tell him. 'I can do it myself.'

Water

is one of

The Elements

Read Evan's story in

Earth

Published by Doubleday
in May 2024

John Boyne is the author of fourteen novels for adults, six for younger readers, and a collection of short stories. His 2006 novel *The Boy in the Striped Pyjamas* has sold more than eleven million copies worldwide and has been adapted for cinema, theatre, ballet and opera. He has won four Irish Book Awards, including Author of the Year in 2022, along with a host of other international literary prizes. His novels are published in fifty-nine languages, making him the most translated Irish writer of all time.

Twitter: @JohnBoyneBooks
Instagram: @JohnBoyneAuthor